Praise for

ZACK AND THE TURKEY ATTACK!

"This funny, engrossing mystery . . .
serves up an intriguing puzzle, a vivid
setting, well-rounded characters, and
a cheer-worthy conclusion."
—*BOOKLIST*

"Charming and lighthearted."
—*KIRKUS REVIEWS*

"A homespun novel underscoring
the importance of family and friends."
—*PUBLISHERS WEEKLY*

"Light and humorous."
—*SCHOOL LIBRARY JOURNAL*

ALSO BY PHYLLIS REYNOLDS NAYLOR

SHILOH BOOKS
Shiloh • Shiloh Season • Saving Shiloh • A Shiloh Christmas

THE ALICE BOOKS
*Starting with Alice • Alice in Blunderland
Lovingly Alice • The Agony of Alice
Alice in Rapture, Sort Of • Reluctantly Alice
All But Alice • Alice in April
Alice In-Between • Alice the Brave
Alice in Lace • Outrageously Alice
Achingly Alice • Alice on the Outside
The Grooming of Alice • Alice Alone
Simply Alice • Patiently Alice
Including Alice • Alice on Her Way
Alice in the Know • Dangerously Alice
Almost Alice • Intensely Alice
Alice in Charge • Incredibly Alice
Alice on Board • Now, I'll Tell You Everything*

ALICE COLLECTIONS
*I Like Him, He Likes Her
It's Not Like I Planned It This Way
Please Don't Be True
You and Me and the Space In Between*

THE BERNIE MAGRUDER BOOKS
*Bernie Magruder and the Case of the Big Stink
Bernie Magruder and the Disappearing Bodies
Bernie Magruder and the Haunted Hotel
Bernie Magruder and the Drive-thru Funeral Parlor
Bernie Magruder and the Bus Station Blowup
Bernie Magruder and the Pirate's Treasure
Bernie Magruder and the Parachute Peril
Bernie Magruder and the Bats in the Belfry*

THE CAT PACK BOOKS

The Grand Escape • *The Healing of Texas Jake*
Carlotta's Kittens • *Polo's Mother*

THE YORK TRILOGY

Shadows on the Wall • *Faces in the Water*
Footprints at the Window

THE WITCH BOOKS

Witch's Sister • *Witch Water*
The Witch Herself • *The Witch's Eye*
Witch Weed • *The Witch Returns*

PICTURE BOOKS

King of the Playground
The Boy with the Helium Head
Old Sadie and the Christmas Bear
Keeping a Christmas Secret • *Ducks Disappearing*
I Can't Take You Anywhere • *Sweet Strawberries*
Please DO Feed the Bears

BOOKS FOR YOUNG READERS

Josie's Troubles • *How Lazy Can You Get?*
All Because I'm Older • *Maudie in the Middle*
One of the Third-Grade Thonkers • *Roxie and the Hooligans*

BOOKS FOR MIDDLE READERS

How I Came to Be a Writer
Eddie, Incorporated • *The Solomon System*
Night Cry • *Beetles, Lightly Toasted* • *The Fear Place*
Being Danny's Dog • *Danny's Desert Rats*

BOOKS FOR OLDER READERS

Walking Through the Dark • *A String of Chances*
The Dark of the Tunnel • *The Year of the Gopher* • *Ice*
Send No Blessings • *Sang Spell* • *The Keeper* • *Walker's Crossing*
Jade Green • *Blizzard's Wake* • *Cricket Man*

ZACK AND THE TURKEY ATTACK!

PHYLLIS REYNOLDS NAYLOR

Illustrations by Vivienne To

A CAITLYN DLOUHY BOOK

Atheneum Books for Young Readers
New York   London   Toronto   Sydney   New Delhi

ATHENEUM BOOKS FOR YOUNG READERS
An imprint of Simon & Schuster Children's Publishing Division
1230 Avenue of the Americas, New York, New York 10020
This book is a work of fiction. Any references to historical events, real people, or real places are used fictitiously. Other names, characters, places, and events are products of the author's imagination, and any resemblance to actual events or places or persons, living or dead, is entirely coincidental.
Text copyright © 2017 by Phyllis Reynolds Naylor
Illustrations copyright © 2017 by Vivienne To
All rights reserved, including the right of reproduction in whole or in part in any form.
Atheneum Books for Young Readers is a registered trademark of Simon & Schuster, Inc.
Atheneum logo is a trademark of Simon & Schuster, Inc.
For information about special discounts for bulk purchases, please contact Simon & Schuster Special Sales at 1-866-506-1949 or business@simonandschuster.com.
The Simon & Schuster Speakers Bureau can bring authors to your live event. For more information or to book an event, contact the Simon & Schuster Speakers Bureau at 1-866-248-3049 or visit our website at www.simonspeakers.com.
Also available in an Atheneum Books for Young Readers hardcover edition
Cover design by Russell Gordon, interior design by Mike Rosamilia
The text for this book was set in Excelsior LT Std.
The illustrations for this book were rendered digitally.
Manufactured in the United States of America
0818 OFF
First Atheneum Books for Young Readers paperback edition September 2018
2 4 6 8 10 9 7 5 3 1
The Library of Congress has cataloged the hardcover edition as follows:
Names: Naylor, Phyllis Reynolds, author. | To, Vivienne, illustrator.
Title: Zack and the turkey attack! / Phyllis Reynolds Naylor ; illustrated by Vivienne To.
Description: First Edition. | New York : Atheneum Books for Young Readers, [2017] | "A Caitlyn Dlouhy Book."
Identifiers: LCCN 2017022130| ISBN 9781481437790 (hardback) | ISBN 9781481437806 (paperback) | ISBN 9781481437813 (eBook)
Subjects: | CYAC: Turkeys—Fiction. | Lost and found possessions—Fiction. | Farm life—Fiction. | Inventions—Fiction. | Mystery and detective stories. | BISAC: JUVENILE FICTION / Social Issues / Friendship. | JUVENILE FICTION / Animals / Birds. | JUVENILE FICTION / Mysteries & Detective Stories.
Classification: LCC PZ7.N24 Zac 2017 | DDC [Fic]—dc23
LC record available at https://lccn.loc.gov/2017022130

For my grandson Beckett
—P. R. N.

CONTENTS

ONE.......................... *Turkey Trouble*

TWO....................... *Nosy Josie*

THREE .... *Missing*

FOUR...................... *Trapped*

FIVE .... *Walking the Plank*

SIX.......................... *Pickup Sticks*

SEVEN.................... *The Bicycle Move*

EIGHT...................... *Company*

NINE........................ *A Bad Idea*

TEN .... *The Waiting Game*

ELEVEN .... *Show Me*

TWELVE .... *Moving Day*

THIRTEEN .... *Down the Rain Gutter*

FOURTEEN .... *Matthew at Night*

FIFTEEN .... *In the Moonlight*

SIXTEEN .... *XPA 5*

SEVENTEEN .... *Testing, Testing . . .*

EIGHTEEN .... *Picture Time*

NINETEEN .... *The Turkey-Blaster Trouble-Shooter*

One

TURKEY TROUBLE

Zack climbed out of the pickup truck, his heart beating fast. He was wearing the Denver Broncos T-shirt he'd got for his ninth birthday, but this morning it didn't help. He wondered if he should make a run for it. Somewhere, the turkey was waiting.

Maybe it was the noise of the truck.

Maybe it was the little tap of the horn.

Or perhaps it was just pure meanness that made the old tom turkey chase Zack and peck at his legs each time he came to his grandparents' farm.

"Hi, Mom!" his dad called as Grandma came out on the back porch.

Zack looked quickly around and took a step forward. Then another.

Suddenly, from behind an azalea bush, a huge turkey came charging across the yard, wings flapping, feathers flying. It lowered its head, loud gobbling noises coming from its throat. And as Zack ran, he felt a nip on his calf, then another—a tug on his jeans.

"Oww! Get *away*!" Zack yelled, but the turkey kept coming, kept pecking, until Zack reached the steps of the farmhouse and Dad swooped his arms at the bird, driving him back into the clearing.

"That Old Tom!" Grandma said. "He thinks he owns the place."

Old Tailpipe—that was *Zack's* name for him, because he was always right behind you and made as much noise as a tailpipe without a muffler.

"Better bring a squirt bottle next time, Zack," Dad said, laughing. "Get that turkey right between the eyes."

Inside the kitchen, Zack sat down on a chair and rubbed his leg. It wasn't funny.

"That old gobbler get you again?" asked Grandpa, looking up from his breakfast. "If the hens wouldn't miss him, I'd roast him up for Sunday dinner. Gets meaner every year."

"Now that our Trixie is gone, Old Tom thinks he's a watchdog," said Grandma, motioning for Zack's dad to sit, then passing a platter of eggs and sausage around the table, followed by a stack of apple pancakes. "He can't bark, so he chases after everyone who comes to the farm."

The grown-ups treated it as though it was just a part of farm life. No big deal.

"He doesn't peck at you or Grandpa," said Zack. "He doesn't peck Dad."

"And he'd better not, or he's turkey soup,"

3

said Grandpa, with a wink. "No, he just goes after small fry. Must think you're another gobbler, come to take his place. You've got to show Old Tom who's boss, that's all."

Easy for you to say, Zack thought as he stabbed his fork into one of the fat sausages, then smeared a thick pat of butter over his pancakes. Grandpa was a lot taller than he was and twice as round.

Zack's family used to live in the city, but a few months ago they had moved closer to Grandma and Grandpa to help out on the farm. Gramps had given Dad the used pickup truck to run errands for him—to buy sacks of feed for the hens and trays of new baby chicks in the spring. Every weekend, when Zack and Dad drove over, the visit began with a good dinner, if it was Friday and they stayed overnight, or a big breakfast, if they came on Saturday.

Zack liked his grandma's cooking, and he

especially liked all the mechanical outdoors stuff—the milking machine, the tractor, the hay baler, and the ride over in the pickup. But Tailpipe was always there to meet them and went after Zack first thing.

"I don't see why you're afraid of an old turkey," his friend Matthew had said just the week before, when Zack told him about it. "It's only a big bird."

"You've never seen *this* turkey!" said Zack. "He's a monster, and his beak is as sharp as a nut pick!"

"Then what you need," Matthew had said, "is to turn around and chase *him* for a change."

Yeah, right, Zack thought now as he cut his sausage into little pieces and dipped each one in syrup. It was simple talking about what you'd do to old Tailpipe until he was right behind you, *peck, peck, pecking* at your legs, your clothes, your butt. And today, Zack was going to stay as far from that turkey as he could get.

Two

NOSY JOSIE

"**W**hat jobs do you want me to do first?" Zack asked his grandmother when he had finished his pancakes.

Grandma reached in her shirt pocket and pulled out a list. She had a list for everything. *Everything.* Zack felt sure that her list began each morning with, *Number One: Wake up.*

"I'd like you to water all the flowers on the porch," Grandma began. "Then I want you to check the fence around my vegetable garden and find the place where the turkey's getting in. That Old Tom is scratching

6

and digging up my plants before they have a chance to grow."

"I'll find it," Zack said, hoping Tailpipe didn't find him first.

"And finally," Grandma went on, "I want you to search the haymow and see if the hens have laid any eggs in there. After that, you can have the rest of the morning to do whatever you like." Then she added, "Josie was asking about you last week. I told her you'd be coming this Saturday."

Zack didn't want to hear that. Josie Wells was from the neighboring farm. She was okay, but he didn't want her around right now. When he got back home, Matthew would ask him right off what he had done about the turkey, and Zack wanted to have a plan. Nosy Josie asked too many questions, and Zack needed time to think.

Last weekend she wanted to know his middle name. The Saturday before that, she

7

asked which he liked best: bananas or pears. The time before that, she asked if he'd ever broken a leg. *Did you ever get stung by a hornet? Get your finger caught in a door? Can you tell a raspberry from a blackberry with your eyes closed? Which is better— vanilla or butter pecan?*

Zack picked up the watering can and went out to the white-and-purple petunias on the front porch. As he watered each pot, he decided to make a map of the whole farm. He would figure out all the different ways he could get from one place to another without running into Tailpipe.

From here, he could see out across the bright-green lawn and Grandma's vegetable garden beyond it. To the left was the grove of evergreen trees that protected the house from prairie winds. To the right was the long lane that led out to the mailbox by the road.

When he went to the back porch and stood at the screen, the old red barn was straight ahead. To the left of the barn were the pigsty and cow pasture. To the right were the silo, the tractor shed, the machine shack, and the chicken coop.

But just outside the back steps was "the clearing"—a large bare space mostly clear of worn-down grass where Dad parked his pickup truck and Grandma parked her car— where feet went back and forth from house to barn to tractor shed many times a day. Beyond it all—the garden, the barn, the silo, the machine shack—were the wheat and soybean fields where Dad and Grandpa spent most of their time.

It was the clearing that Tailpipe liked best—strutting about, watching the hens, and looking for someone to peck. If Zack could figure out ways to get from one place to another without crossing the clearing, he

9

would have a lot more fun when he came to the farm on weekends.

He waited until he saw the old gobbler wander off toward the evergreens behind the house, and then Zack headed for the vegetable garden. He walked all around it. Sure enough, there was the place the wire had given way; a turkey or anything else could walk right through. Zack stuck a stick in the wire so Grandma would know where to look when she came to fix it.

Then he went to the barn. Opening the big double doors, he stared into the darkness, drinking in the smell of warm hay, of cows and cats and mice. *Our old-timey farm,* Grandpa had said, because he still kept some hay in there. *A grandfolksy kind of place,* Grandma called it, because they still had a pump on their back porch. Zack was glad the farm was old-timey and grandfolksy, because this was the way he liked it. If only it didn't have a tom turkey.

He walked over to the huge tower of hay in one corner and began to climb. The hay scrunched underfoot, and Zack sank down a few inches with each step. But he continued the climb, scrambling to the very top of the pile under the eaves.

There were cobwebs among the rafters, and an old nest that the sparrows had built. Sometimes hens came into the barn and laid their eggs up here near the roof. This time Zack found two eggs. Holding them gently, one in each hand, he slid back down the haystack, dust rising to his nostrils.

The four cows were out to pasture, their stalls empty. Cats moved around the open doorway, yawning in the sun. Zack peered cautiously out, and seeing the turkey leading the hens back into the clearing, he sat down on a barrel and waited five or six minutes until it had ambled behind the chicken coop.

Zack made a run for the house. He gave the eggs to his grandmother and then, sneaking back to the barn, he went through the cow gate into the pasture and walked as far as the plum tree. Following the fence till he was way past the barn, past the silo, he kept circling around until he thought he saw the stand of evergreen trees far ahead, which meant the house must be somewhere up there.

This was sure a long way to go to get from the barn to the house without crossing the clearing, but he could do it. Now to work out some other paths. Zack made his way around a thicket of wild blueberries, and suddenly he came face-to-face with Josie Wells on the other side of the fence. One minute he was looking at blueberry bushes and the next minute he was looking at two green eyes above a wide smile that turned down a little at the corners.

"Hi, Zack!" she said. "Guess what? My brother's home from the navy, and he's got an apartment in town."

"That's good," said Zack, and kept walking.

"He's going to school, but he'll help out here now and then," said Josie, following along on the other side of the fence.

"Cool," said Zack.

"Want to come over and hang out on the tire swing?"

Zack shook his head. "Not today."

"Want to wade in the creek?"

"Some other time," he told her.

"Want to look at a dead raccoon?"

"No," Zack told her. "I'm thinking."

Josie didn't take no for an answer. "What about?" she asked, and her dark ponytail bobbed up and down with each step.

When he didn't reply, she said, "If I guess, will you tell me?" When he still didn't answer, she said, "Skunks? The ones that got under the barn?"

Zack shook his head.

"NASCAR?"

"Nope."

"Chocolate chunk cookies?"

"No," said Zack. "And I have to get back now." He was trying to remember how many turns he had made.

"Wait!" Josie reached out and tugged at his sleeve. "I have to show you something first."

Zack stopped. Josie's smile had disappeared. "What is it?" he asked.

"You have to see for yourself," Josie said mysteriously, "because *it* could happen to *you*!"

Three

MISSING

Zack didn't want to go to Josie's place— he wanted to make his map. But if something else was about to happen to him— something *bad*—he needed to know.

Josie waited, hands on her hips, as Zack swung one leg over the top of the wood fence, then the other, and jumped down.

"Yesterday," she told him as they started through the cornfield toward the Wellses' farmhouse, "my mom's gold bracelet disappeared."

"You mean, one minute it was there and then it wasn't?" Zack asked.

"No. I mean that's when she discovered it was gone. And I wasn't even wearing it. I'm only allowed to wear it in the house because it could slip right off."

"So what do you guess happened to it?" said Zack.

"Mom thinks I lost it," said Josie. "I *told* her I hadn't even tried on that bracelet for . . . Well, maybe I did try it on, but I hadn't worn it. . . . Well, maybe I did wear it just a little around the house, but I've never—*hardly* ever—worn it outside."

Zack wished he hadn't climbed the fence. Wished he had just kept going. He wasn't much interested in gold bracelets.

Josie tugged at his sleeve again. "Do you know how much that bracelet cost?"

Zack shook his head.

"It's priceless! Mom said that all the money

16

in the world wouldn't pay for it, because Dad gave it to her on their honeymoon."

They left the cornfield and walked across the yard to her house. Josie led him around to the side. "Look," she said.

Zack looked where she was pointing. All he could see were a few mashed petunias beneath a window.

"*What?*" he said.

Josie stepped closer to the house, still pointing. "Footprints!" This time her eyes were as large as coat buttons. "*Big* ones!"

Zack could see them now—two big footprints with V-shaped treads, right in the middle of the smashed-down petunias. "So?" he said.

"Don't you *see*? Somebody was here at the window, and *I* think that somebody climbed in and took Mom's bracelet."

"Why do you think that?"

"Because there's a robber out here! The

Smiths and the Baileys and the Hendersons have all had things missing, so it probably means that your grandparents' farm is next."

"Grandma doesn't wear gold bracelets," said Zack.

"It could be anything!" said Josie, and then her voice became low and mysterious. "The Smiths lost their snowblower. At the Baileys' it was an angel food cake, and a pig is missing at the Hendersons'."

Now it was beginning to sound serious. "And they haven't found the person who took the stuff?" Zack asked.

Josie's eyes narrowed to tiny slits. "*Ne-ver*," she said. "Which means he's still around, waiting to strike."

Zack's heart began to thump a little faster. "How do you know it was a *he*? What would a man want with a gold bracelet?"

"To sell it!" said Josie, and pointed to the footprints again. "Those are the deep

19

footprints of somebody heavy. I'm just saying that you had better keep your eye out for anyone creeping or sneaking around your grandparents' place after dark."

Zack felt a slight shiver run down his spine. "I will," he said.

Josie thrust her hands in her pockets and dropped her head. "Mom's bracelet is probably gone forever," she said in a small voice.

"Maybe your brother will find the burglar and get the bracelet back before it's sold," Zack offered.

The corners of Josie's mouth turned down. "Adam said he'd keep an eye out. But if he doesn't get it back, Mom will think that I'm the one who lost it, and she'll be mad at me for the rest of my life."

"Nobody stays mad that long," Zack said. "Anyway, I'll look for burglars sneaking around our place." He thought again of the map he was going to make and the number of turns he had made already. Was it three or four? "I need to get back," he said. "I'll come over some other time."

"I'll go with you as far as the fence," said Josie, and walked along beside him.

Here come the questions, Zack thought.

"Want to know the craziest thing I ever did?" Josie asked. And without waiting for an answer, she said, "I rode my belly board down the creek when the water was high."

"How far did you get?" Zack asked.

"Not very. I crashed where the creek makes the turn. What's the craziest thing *you* ever did?"

"Um . . . I took my sister's little sewing machine apart once and couldn't get it back together again," said Zack. "I just wanted to see how it worked."

"I'll bet *she* was mad!" said Josie.

"Sounded like a fire siren going off, the

way she yelled," Zack told her, and that made both of them smile.

They reached the fence and Zack climbed over.

"Well, bye," Josie said. "Look out for burglars."

"Bye," he told her. Now there were *two* things to look out for here at the farm, Zack was thinking when he finally reached the road. Pretty soon he was starting up the lane toward the house. Well, if a burglar *did* come creeping or crawling, sneaking or stalking around his grandfather's place looking for something to steal, Zack thought, he hoped he'd take the turkey.

When he got to the lawn, he sighed: halfway between him and the house was old Tailpipe.

Four

TRAPPED

Zack stood still as a stone.

Tailpipe was pecking in the dirt, the red wattle beneath his beak swinging back and forth. Then he stopped pecking and started scratching instead. His long yellow claws looked like eagle talons, and Zack swallowed.

A whole minute passed, maybe two. Zack didn't move a muscle. He wondered if Tailpipe could hear him breathing.

But then Zack noticed something else. With a couple of hens behind him, the big turkey kept coming slowly toward him, pecking at the grass all the while, not even realizing that Zack was there. Maybe turkeys couldn't see as well as they could run. Maybe Tailpipe thought Zack was a fence post. Maybe he thought he was a tree.

Now the turkey was only ten feet away . . . nine feet away. Zack's heart beat faster, and a trickle of sweat ran down his back.

He and Tailpipe had never been this close before, except when the turkey was chasing him. The bird was truly monstrous, at least four feet long from the end of his beak to the tip of his tail feathers. Every so often he gobbled to the hens, spreading his wings, showing off his black and red and green feathers in front, the brown and white in back. Grandpa called him a Bronze turkey. Zack called him *scary*.

The turkey must have come across a whole bunch of bugs, because he clucked again, loud this time, and the hens came hurrying over. *Peck . . . peck . . . peck . . .* Their heads moved up and down like pump handles as they enjoyed their lunch.

Tailpipe had his back to Zack now. Maybe, just maybe, Zack thought, he could move a few feet at a time and slowly . . . slowly . . . get over to the porch. Maybe the old gobbler and his hens wouldn't notice that the fence post was moving.

Zack took one step to the side and stopped. Tailpipe lifted his head for a moment, one dark eye staring off to the left. Zack froze. But after a moment the pecking began again, and Zack dared a second step, a big one.

This time, the turkey saw.

The tail feathers spread. The wings flapped. The yellow feet moved, and Tailpipe came straight at Zack. In fact, he was between Zack and the house, pecking at him furiously.

Zack ran for the pickup truck, but he knew that in the time it would take to get the door open and climb up, the turkey would be on top of him.

The barn was too far away and the tractor shed was open at both ends. The only place left to hide was the machine shack where Grandpa stored his junk.

Zack raced to the open doorway, ducked inside, and yanked the crooked door closed behind him, almost catching the turkey in it.

Tailpipe gobbled loudly and pecked hard at the door. *You may be fast, but you're stupid,* Zack thought. When the pecking stopped, the gobbler didn't go away, however. Through a crack in the wall, Zack could see him strutting back and forth, head jerking forward and each foot lifting high off the ground with each step.

Trapped. Zack's breathing slowed a little because he knew he was safe, but could he get out? At some point, Tailpipe would give up and go back to the hens, but when? Would the turkey still be here at lunchtime? Would Dad have to come looking for him when it was time to go home?

He rubbed his arm where the turkey had pecked him and noticed it was bleeding a little. Then he saw blood on his shirt. And *then* he realized that Tailpipe had pecked a hole in his new Denver Broncos T-shirt.

That did it! Never mind a map of the farm! Never mind secret paths that didn't cross the clearing! Zack was going to get even if it was the last thing he did. He wasn't sure how, but he'd think of something.

He sat down on a dusty stool and wiped his arm again. He thought about just going out there and charging at the turkey, the way Matthew said to do, yelling and waving his arms like Dad did. Chasing Tailpipe before the turkey could chase him.

But then he remembered the time a neighbor had stopped by the farm with his dog. A big dog. The dog had seen Tailpipe across the barnyard and run toward him, barking. And before anyone could say *drumstick*, the turkey charged at the dog—a blur of feathers and feet—and the dog had gone racing back to its master, tail between its legs. Zack knew exactly who would do the running if *he* tried to chase the turkey. Looked like he was stuck here for a few hours.

He stood up and poked around the machine shack, looking at all Grandpa's stuff, the things he didn't use anymore. They were piled all over the top of the workbench as well as below it, and along the walls. They hung from hooks, weighted down shelves, and half covered the one small window.

There were old broken-down machines and parts of engines. The wringer from an old-fashioned washing machine, the crank from a butter churn, a rusty saw. There was a lamp without a shade, a wagon without a wheel, an old sewing machine, and a croquet game with broken mallets. Pieces of rain gutters, parts of a bike. Zack's eyes traveled from shelf to shelf, hook to hook, box to box, and barrel to barrel. He could take this old sewing machine apart and nobody would care whether he got it back together or not. There weren't any big machines out here, but a lot of machine parts.

And suddenly Zack had an idea. That old turkey was nothing but trouble, and he was going to build a trouble-shooter. A turkey-blaster trouble-shooter. Something that would scare old Tailpipe right out of his feathers.

Five

WALKING THE PLANK

When Zack's dad finally came looking for him later, and the two of them rode home, Zack walked down to Matthew's house and told him about being trapped in the machine shack. He described all the weird stuff he had found there, and how Tailpipe paced and pecked outside the door. Matthew was the first friend Zack had made when his family moved to the new house, closer to the farm.

"What you need," said Matthew, "is an explosion."

"You mean, blow up the turkey?" asked Zack. He wasn't ready to go that far.

"Not exactly. But you can't go around being scared of a bird all the time."

The two boys were sitting on Zack's back porch eating chocolate cake. Emilene, Zack's sister, who was only a year younger, had celebrated her birthday with some of her friends that afternoon. Pink and white balloons were everywhere.

There was leftover strawberry ice cream in bowls, melted, of course, and leftover pink lemonade in cups. Even the frosting on the leftover cake was pink. Zack was glad he and his dad hadn't gotten back until all the girls had gone home, and now there was all this leftover stuff to eat. He wiped one finger along the plate and scooped up the extra frosting.

"So what kind of machine do you want to build?" Matthew asked, when Zack told him about wanting to get even with Tailpipe.

"Something big and noisy that will make that turkey jump three feet in the air and never come near me again," said Zack.

Matthew rested his chin in his hands and thought for a minute. His face was as long and narrow as Zack's was round, and he had dark-blue eyes that seemed to flash when he had an idea. At last he said, "Let's start with 'walk the plank.'"

Zack stared at him. "Like . . . pirates on a ship?"

"Sort of," said Matthew.

"We're going to *drown* the turkey?"

"No. Just listen. Have you got a plank? A board? Any old board?"

Zack hopped off the porch and went across the yard to the garage. The previous owner had left some of his own junk in the garage, and Zack found a long strip of wood. It was only four inches wide and wasn't very strong, but he brought it back to the porch.

When he went up the steps, he saw that Matthew had pulled down a bunch of balloons and placed them in a row along the floor.

"See if you can hold them still," Matthew said, and took the strip of wood from Zack, laying it carefully on top of the five balloons. "Now," he said, "walk the plank and see if we get an explosion."

Zack knew what would happen, but he did it anyway. He lifted his right foot and stepped on one end of the board.

BAM! went the first balloon.

Zack took another step.

BAM! BAM! went two more.

Just as the fourth balloon was popping, Emilene came running out onto the porch in her new pink-and-purple sneakers.

"What are you *doing*?" she shrieked, and

her voice sounded like a whistle factory blowing up.

"Walking the plank," Zack told her.

"You jerk!" said Emilene. "Those are my *birthday* balloons."

"You've only got a million more," said Zack. "We were just doing an experiment."

"Well, I'm just glad you were at Grandpa and Grandma's today and not here to ruin my party," said Emilene. She gathered up all the other balloons, and with them bumping and bobbing around her head, she marched back into the house.

Matthew looked at Zack and grinned. "That was an explosion, all right!" he said.

"But how do I turn all this into a machine?" asked Zack. "You should come to the farm with me some weekend when we stay overnight and help build it."

"Well, maybe," said Matthew. "How badly do you want to hurt this turkey?"

Zack actually hadn't thought about hurting Tailpipe at all—only scaring him half to death.

"I just want to build some kind of trouble-shooter that will make him stop pecking my legs and ripping my clothes," Zack told him.

"Yeah, but what if we built something that killed him?" said Matthew. "You've got to think what would happen then."

So Zack did think about it—all the next week. If he accidentally killed the turkey and Gramps was right, the hens would miss him. Zack imagined that the next time he came to the farm, he would climb out of the pickup truck, and fourteen hen turkeys would come flying at him, pecking right through his clothes—a thousand peck marks—and he'd never be able to visit his grandparents again.

Six

PICKUP STICKS

The next Saturday, when it was time to go, Zack called Matthew and invited him to come along.

"Oh . . . uh . . . I don't think so," said Matthew. "I've got a sore leg."

"You sprain it or something?" Zack asked.

"I guess," Matthew said.

Zack had seen him the day before, and he'd looked fine.

"Well, next week, then," Zack told him.

"Sure," said Matthew.

This time Zack got a squirt bottle and held

it under the faucet until it was filled to the top. Then he put the cap on it and ran outside to the pickup, where his dad was waiting.

"I think your mom and sister like it when we're gone," Dad said as they rode along the highway. "It gives them time to do things together. And we get to do guy stuff."

"Yeah!" said Zack. "I think I like the farm better than Emilene does."

"Well, she has her cornet lessons and gymnastics practice on Saturdays," Dad said. "What do *you* do all day when Grandpa and I are out with the tractor?"

"Climb the plum tree," said Zack. "Play in the haystack. Fool around in the machine shack."

"Same kinds of things I liked to do when I was your age," said Dad, and chuckled. "A farm is a great place to grow up."

But it would be even better if there wasn't a turkey on it, Zack thought.

When they pulled into the clearing, Zack looked all around before he got out of the pickup. He put one foot on the ground. Then the other. He had the squirt bottle in his hands, one finger on the button. But the turkey was nowhere in sight, and this time Zack got safely into the house without getting pecked.

Grandma had biscuits with honey butter and blackberry jam waiting for him.

"Josie was looking for you early this morning," she told Zack. "She wanted to wade in the creek. I think she's trying to catch tadpoles. Wouldn't you like to do that?"

Zack would, but not today. "I'll help some other time," he answered. The sooner he could build a turkey-blaster trouble-shooter, the better. Josie would just want to talk about burglars.

Halfway through breakfast, there was a knock at the door and Grandpa answered it. When he came back into the kitchen, a tall young man in jeans and an orange plaid shirt was with him.

"Adam!" cried Grandma, coming over to give the young man a hug.

"Zack, this is Josie's brother, Adam, home from the navy," Grandpa said. "Came by to say hello, and it's sure nice to have him back."

"How ya doin'?" Adam said, smiling at Zack, and he reached out to shake hands. Adam's hand seemed as big as a catcher's mitt.

"Hi," said Zack.

"How does it feel to be out of uniform?" Grandma asked.

"Feels pretty darn good," said Adam. "I'll be heading into town to move some of my stuff to an apartment, and I wondered if I could pick up anything for you while I'm there."

"Well, I could use a couple of things

from the Safeway, but not until you sit down and have some breakfast with us," Grandma said.

"Hey, I've already had one breakfast," Adam said.

"Why, I've never known you to refuse my biscuits," said Grandma. "I remember once, when you were sixteen or so, you ate nearly a half dozen, one right after the other."

Adam laughed. "Yeah, they called me 'chowhound' in the navy, too, but I'll have to save that biscuit for another time. Got two loads of stuff to move today. Glad I found an apartment near the college when school starts this fall. Now what do you need from the Safeway?"

Zack was happy that Adam hadn't stayed for breakfast, because he and his father ate every last biscuit on the table.

Afterward, Grandma had a new job for Zack. She handed him a trash basket and asked him to pick up all the sticks in the yard so they wouldn't get caught in the mower.

With his squirt bottle in one hand, Zack went out on the front porch and surveyed the area. He was happy to see that the turkey was off by the pasture for a change. So he lugged the trash basket into the yard and hunkered down to pick up sticks.

It had been windy the day before, and the yard was full of small branches and twigs. If Matthew had come, they could have done this job in half the time, Zack thought. But he put his mind to thinking about the trouble-shooter he wanted to build. He figured it would have to be a machine with wheels so he could move it around and point it in any direction. You never knew where the turkey would come from next.

Sometimes the turkey came at him when he got out of the truck. Sometimes it came at him when he walked to the barn. Sometimes it surprised him out by the henhouse, and sometimes it seemed to be waiting just for him in front of the porch. But it spent most of the day in the clearing where it was easiest to scratch for bugs.

There were more sticks than Zack had expected, and Grandma had more trees than he remembered. He wouldn't care if Josie Wells came along just then to help out.

But Josie didn't come. The turkey came.

Just when Zack quit worrying about Tailpipe and tried to guess how long it would take him to finish the yard, he heard that low *gobble, gobble* sound. The next thing he knew, a big ball of brown and red feathers was coming right at him.

Seven

THE BICYCLE MOVE

Zack dropped the trash basket and reached for the squirt bottle on the grass. But before he could squeeze the handle, the turkey flew straight at him, knocking him over.

Peck, peck, peck. Zack felt the sharp stabs on his arms, his chest. *Arrrghh!* He managed to raise the squirt bottle and squeeze. The water hit Tailpipe on one wing.

Again! *Squirt! Squirt!*

This time the stream of water hit the old gobbler just below one eye, but it didn't even slow him down.

Peck, peck, peck. Zack lay on the ground, kicking wildly with both feet and yelling at him. It was only then that the turkey moved away, but he stood close by, just waiting for an opening to attack again.

This is ridiculous, Zack thought as he lay on the ground, his feet pedaling an invisible bicycle in the air. Was this what he had to do whenever Tailpipe came at him? Roll over on his back and kick his feet?

Finally the turkey got tired of waiting around and strutted off to where the hens were scratching for bugs in the dirt.

Zack lowered his legs and lay there in the grass, staring up at the tree branches.

When he built his machine, his turkey-blaster trouble-shooter, it was going to go wherever he wanted. It was going to make really loud noises, and shoot out stuff, and roll and rattle and make that stupid gobbler think twice before pecking him again.

Zack sat up finally and looked around. When he was sure the turkey was gone, he got to his feet and marched straight to the machine shack, leaving the basket of sticks on the lawn. He'd finish this job later. Right now he had something more important to do.

The old rusty wagon that Zack had noticed before was tucked under the workbench, and he pulled it out. The handle squeaked, but it still turned. If only he could find a spare wheel.

Inside a box on a broken rocking chair, Zack found a lazy Susan, as Grandma called it—a large tin platter that turned around and around. It was the kind of thing you put in the middle of the table with salt and pepper and mustard and ketchup on it. When anyone needed more ketchup, he'd just reach out and whirl the lazy Susan until the ketchup was right in front of him, and no one had to pass it around the table.

The lazy Susan had a dent in one side, which was why it was in the machine shack, waiting for someone to fix it. Zack didn't care about the dent. It still turned. He put it in the wagon. Now, if he could build his trouble-shooter on top of the lazy Susan, he could pull it wherever he needed to go, point it in any direction at all, and fire away. Just let old Tailpipe come at him. Just let him try pecking Zack. One blast from the trouble-shooter and the next time he met Zack, he'd turn his tail feathers around and head for the barn, he'd be so scared. Zack would just have to make sure he didn't kill him.

He stopped suddenly and listened. There was a noise outside the machine shack— the kind of noise a turkey might make if it flapped its wings, trying to scramble its way up the woodpile to see in the little window on one side.

48

The noise stopped. Zack waited. Then it came again—a soft, sliding noise, the kind a burglar might make if he had peeked in the window to see what he might steal, and was trying to get down off the woodpile again.

Zack climbed up on a barrel to see out the dusty window.

Nothing in sight but a few hens pecking around the yard, and a cat lounging in the open doorway of the barn. But somehow a turkey you couldn't see was almost as scary as one right in front of you. You could never tell where it might pop up next. And a burglar could be almost anywhere at all.

Eight

COMPANY

When Grandma rang the bell for lunch, Zack didn't want to stop. He had work to do. He was finding all sorts of things that might be perfect for his trouble-shooter. He'd shaken dirt and spiders out of an old piece of rain gutter. He'd worked the wide pedal of the old sewing machine up and down, and he wanted to try out the handle of an ancient wringer washing machine too. But when he was late for lunch, Grandma's face took on a sour look, so he tried not to let it happen again.

He climbed back over the pile of junk he'd collected and peeked out. No turkey.

With one hand holding onto the door-knob, just in case, Zack took a few steps and looked around the corner of the shack, checking the woodpile.

No turkey. No feathers.

He heard a faraway *gobble, gobble* off in Grandma's garden. Phew. He could make it all the way to the farmhouse without Tailpipe catching him this time.

As he crossed the clearing, he saw the trash basket sitting beside the back steps, and it was packed with sticks. Pieces of small branches were poking out every which way.

Oh no! He had forgotten to finish his job and Grandma had done it herself.

Zack ran up the porch steps, opened the screen, and used the porch pump to wash his hands. Up and down, up and down he pumped the handle. At first no water came out, but when he pumped the third time, he could feel the handle getting harder to push as the pump drew water up from the well. At last it spilled clear and cold into the metal sink. Zack washed his hands, then headed into the big farm kitchen, ready to apologize to Grandma.

Grandpa was sitting at one end of the table, Dad at the other. Grandma sat across from Zack's empty chair, and sitting beside Grandma was . . . Josie Wells. The meal had already begun.

Grandma was frowning, but her face brightened as she passed some ham and beans around the table, and she didn't say a word about the sticks. "Josie's going to eat with us today," she said. "She brought over some flowers from her mother. Aren't they lovely?"

Zack looked at the lavender flowers in the center of the table. Then he looked at the pink freckled face of Josie Wells across from him.

He didn't hate Josie or anything. He didn't even not like her. It was just that he only got to come to the farm once a week, and he didn't want to spend the afternoon with someone else. He wanted to work on his trouble-shooter. But somehow he guessed who had finished picking up those sticks. He ought to thank her, but he didn't.

"Do you like flowers?" Josie asked him.

Zack only shrugged and took a bite of ham.

"Me either," said Josie. "If I had a garden of my own, all I'd plant would be strawberries and popcorn."

"Popcorn!" Zack jeered. "You don't plant popcorn!"

"Of course you do," said Grandpa. "You have to plant a certain kind. Not just any old corn will pop."

Zack hadn't known that. He glanced back at Josie. She was either making a face at him or grinning, he couldn't tell.

Soon the grown-ups were talking about soybeans.

"Looking good," said Zack's dad. "Need a little rain, though."

They went on talking about the potato crop and the new calf and the silo and cistern.

Then Grandma turned to Zack and said, "You and Josie and I are going into the orchard this afternoon and pick some cherries before the birds get them. You ready for some cherry pie, Zack?"

Well, there goes the afternoon, Zack thought, but he was there to help out, after all. Dad didn't bring him to the farm on weekends just to fool around. So he managed a smile at Grandma and said, "Sure." And when lunch was over, he carried one end of the stepladder, Josie carried

54

the other, and they followed Grandma out to the orchard.

It was a fun job, actually. Zack and Josie took turns climbing to the top of the ladder while Grandma held it steady. If Josie was up high doing the picking, Zack held the bucket below and rescued any that fell on the ground when she dropped them.

"We'll do this tree and maybe the next one," Grandma said, popping one of the dark, sweet cherries in her mouth. "Ummmm. Just taste the sweetness. We might even pick enough for me to make some preserves too."

Zack liked being near the top of the ladder. He was high enough that he could see the cows in the pasture . . . could even see the top of the silo over at Josie Wells's place.

"You kids are being a big help to me today," Grandma said. "And thank you for picking up all those sticks this morning, Zack. We had quite a wind last night."

Zack glanced down at Josie and saw that familiar wide smile. He'd better remember to thank her before she went home.

When they had picked the best cherries on two of the trees, Grandma took the half-filled bucket with her and told them to put the stepladder back on the porch. Zack and Josie stayed a few minutes longer to look for any cherries they might have missed on the ground. Then they folded up the ladder, and, each carrying one end of it, they ambled back toward the house.

"Thanks for finishing up the yard for me," Zack told Josie. "I should have told Grandma you did it."

"It's okay. I figured you were busy," Josie told him. And when he didn't say more, she added, "I've been pretty busy too. I've got some detective work to do, because the burglar is back, and this time it happened here."

Zack stopped walking, making the ladder jerk, and turned around. "How do you know?" he asked.

"Your grandma told me. Well, she didn't exactly tell me. But she said that one of her silver earrings is missing, and she didn't realize it till this morning."

"Why would a burglar take only one?" Zack said, slowly moving forward again, and Josie, at the other end of the ladder, followed behind.

"To make it look like she'd just lost it," Josie answered. "Someday he'll come back and get the other one. That's the way burglars work. They're clever."

"Did you tell Gram about your mom's bracelet that's missing?" Zack asked.

Josie shook her head. "I didn't want to scare her. I need more proof. But we've got to keep our eyes open, Zack. Tell me every single thing that goes missing at your grandma's house and I'll tell you what's missing from mine."

"Okay," Zack said.

They reached the house and got the stepladder inside, propped against one wall of the back porch. Then Josie said good-bye, and Zack watched her heading for the shortcut home through the evergreen trees, hands in her pockets, eyes on the ground. Every so often she kicked at something with the toe of her shoe or bent down to examine the grass.

He went back to the machine shack to sort through boxes and barrels, looking for stuff he could use.

Gobble, gobble, gobble came the turkey, grumbling from outside the door, just waiting for Zack to come out so he could peck him.

"You'll have to peck at something else," Zack called out. "I'm busy."

He stopped working suddenly as a new thought came to him. How was it that Josie got around the farm without the turkey chasing *her*? He'd have to ask her sometime.

Nine

A BAD IDEA

"Oh, man!" said Matthew when Zack told him that the squirt bottle hadn't worked to scare the turkey. "What you need is a waterfall."

"A *waterfall*?" Zack exclaimed.

Matthew nodded. He was sprawled on the steps of Zack's front porch, eating a candy bar that stuck to his fingers. "You need something really huge to stop him from chasing you."

"Well, so far I've got a wagon with a turnaround thing on top where I'll build my trouble-shooter," Zack told him.

Matthew shook his head. "A waterfall. You need a waterfall. You can use the other stuff too, but that old gobbler's got to learn that if he starts pecking on you, he doesn't just get squirted, he gets soaked!"

"How do I make a waterfall?" Zack asked.

"Simple," said Matthew, wiping his hands on his jeans. "Your gramps has a hose, doesn't he?"

"Yeah . . . ," said Zack.

"Does he have a porch with a roof over it?"

Zack nodded. "Two of them, front and back."

"Okay, then, here's the deal. You've got to be somewhere the turkey never goes, but where he can still see you. And what you do is, you drag one end of the hose, with the spray handle turned off, into your grand-parents' house, up the stairs, and over to a front window. You wait till you see the turkey in the yard, then you set the spray handle to 'full force' and let him have it. Yell something so he sees it's you up there. Try this two or three times, and he'll know better than to peck you again."

"And if he tries to come up on the porch and get in the house?" asked Zack.

"That's where the waterfall comes in. Every few seconds you aim the nozzle at the roof so there's a waterfall coming off the edge. But each time you soak him, you have to yell something—'turkey dinner,' maybe. That's important. He'll connect the two in his little bird brain. After a while, all you'll have to do when he starts after you in the yard is yell 'turkey dinner' and he'll run."

"Yeah? How do you know all this?" said Zack.

"Because that's how we trained our cat when we got him," Matthew said. "The vet told us to never let him go out, so I'd open the door and stand just outside with a pitcher of water. The minute he stepped out, I'd dump it on him. After three times, we could leave the door wide open and he'd never even try to go through. Come on, let's try it out!"

Actually, Zack's dad had two long hoses connected together at the water faucet at the side of the house. It didn't have a spray handle on the end, so Matthew said he'd turn the water on once Zack got the hose upstairs.

With one end attached to the faucet, Zack dragged the other end up the porch steps, into the house, up the stairs, into Emilene's bedroom, and over to the window above the front porch. He pushed the nozzle out under the screen so it was pointing straight down at the shingles on the roof.

"Okay, Matthew!" he yelled. "Ready."

He waited, and then he thought the hose jerked a little.

Matthew appeared out on the lawn.

"Can you feel it?" he called up.

"I think it's coming," Zack shouted back, as the hose jerked again.

And then he yelled, "Turkey dinner!" as a gush of water exploded out the end of the hose.

At that very moment his dad came around the other side of the house and Matthew dived headfirst into some bushes.

"Hey!" yelled Zack's dad, as a rush of water cascaded off the porch roof.

Zack couldn't pull the hose back inside because the water was still running. He couldn't leave the hose and go outside to turn the faucet off because the end of the hose might fall back into the room.

"Matthew!" he yelled, but obviously his friend was hiding.

"Zack!" came his mom's voice from downstairs. "What is this hose doing in the hallway?"

And with Dad yelling at him from outside, Mom calling to him from below, Emilene suddenly walked into her bedroom and screamed, "What are you *doing*?"

And then she yelled, "Mom! Zack's watering the roof!"

"Turn that water off immediately!" Mom called.

But first Zack had to push the hose out farther still so it wouldn't slide back in. The end of it flopped this way and that, spraying water out over the yard in all directions.

"Zack!" Dad bellowed, wiping his sleeve across his face. "What's the big idea?"

The water finally went off, but when Zack got the hose outside again, Matthew was nowhere in sight.

"Whatever you were doing up there, stop it!" his dad scolded.

"Don't let me see you bringing a hose in the house again!" said his mom.

"And stay out of my room forever!" said Emilene.

Zack sat on the porch steps, arms crossed, a deep, dark scowl on his face. Finally Matthew came slowly around the corner of the house and sat down beside him.

"Sorry about that," Matthew said. "What you need is—"

"What I need is for you to come out to the farm and work on my machine yourself!" said Zack.

After a long minute, Matthew said, "Okay, I will."

Ten

THE WAITING GAME

The next weekend, however, Matthew told Zack that he had a stomachache and couldn't come. "But the Saturday after this one, I will," he said.

"I don't think so," said Zack. "I don't think you *want* to come."

"I *do*!" said Matthew. "As soon as my stomachache's better, I'll be there."

So once again, Zack and his dad set off for Grandpa's. Matthew, of the Big Ideas, wasn't with them.

This time, when they drove up the lane

where the turkey was waiting, Zack didn't get out his side of the truck. He scooted over into the driver's seat and slid out right after his dad. With his legs as close to his father's as he could get, he took giant steps, just like his dad's, and walked with him up onto the porch.

Tailpipe was confused and complained loudly as he strutted around the truck, looking for a boy to peck.

But Zack didn't want to spend the rest of his life having to slide into the driver's seat to get out of the truck without being pecked. He didn't want to have to lie on his back and kick his feet in the air to keep the turkey off him. He didn't want to be chased by a turkey every time he came to the farm.

Grandma had spent the week making blueberry and cherry preserves. After breakfast, she asked Zack to take her twenty-four jars of jam to the storeroom in the cellar.

Carefully he placed six jars at a time in a box and carried them down the narrow stairs to the damp, dark basement. He lined them up on the shelves along with jars of green lima beans, orange and yellow peppers, red tomatoes, and dark-purple plums. After his fourth trip, he was about to head for the machine shack when Grandma said there was one more job to do.

"Come in here," she called, leading him into the parlor, and there, lying on the rug, was a man. A man made of straw. Part of a man, anyway, because his hands and feet were missing.

"Help me finish this old scarecrow," Grandma said, "and then we'll take him out to my garden and set him up."

Zack grinned. "Okay. What should I do next?"

"Put this old yardstick inside his shirt so that it's holding the sleeves out on both

sides," Grandma said. "Then stuff those old work gloves with straw and we'll pin them to the shirt cuffs. I'll figure out a way to tie your grandpa's old slippers to the bottoms of the trousers. Maybe we can make him look real enough to keep those pesky crows away from my plants."

"Does a scarecrow really work?" Zack asked as he picked up a handful of straw from a basket and pushed it down into the fingers of the raggedy gloves.

"For a while it does, but we'll have to keep moving it around from time to time. Crows are pretty smart, but I'd like to think I'm smarter."

When it was done at last, Zack lifted the scarecrow off the floor, and with Grandma carrying an old broomstick and a hammer, they crossed the front lawn, into Grandma's garden, and found a spot among the new seedlings.

Grandma pounded the end of the broom-stick into the ground until it didn't wiggle much at all. Then Zack slipped the bottom of the scarecrow's shirt over the end of the broomstick, up behind its back and under the old cap on its head.

They both stepped back and looked it over. Grandma had painted a face on the round pillow that formed the head. The cap slouched down over one eye, and one of the gloves, dangling from a sleeve, waved a little in the morning breeze.

"In a week or so, I'll come out and stick a little flag in his hand," said Grandma. "Just to keep the crows guessing."

When Grandma went back into the house, Zack waited till Tailpipe had gone off behind the barn. Then he ran to the machine shack and closed the door.

There was the old wagon, just where he had left it, but something was different. It had a new wheel. Wow! Zack would have to remember to thank Gramps for it at lunch. Now he could pull his trouble-shooter anywhere he needed to go.

He worked all morning. He couldn't figure out how to use the lazy Susan yet, but he nailed an old window screen to the back of the wagon so that it stuck up in the air like a sail. He nailed one end of a piece of rain gutter to the top of the screen. When he dropped a croquet ball down the gutter, it shot out the curved end at the bottom and hit the front rim of the wagon. *Bam!* Zack smiled. This was a start.

When Grandma rang the bell for lunch and Zack sat down at the table with his dad and his grandparents, he said, "Thanks, Gramps, for fixing the wagon."

"What's that?" said Gramps. "What wagon?"

"The one in the machine shack. It's got a new wheel," Zack told him.

"Well, I don't know how that happened, because I don't have an extra wheel, and if I did, I don't have any extra minutes," said Grandpa.

Zack looked at his dad.

"Search me!" said his father. "I don't know anything about a wagon." Grandma didn't say anything, but she was too busy to fool around with a wagon. If she wasn't picking beans, she was weeding. And if she wasn't weeding, she was baking pies or washing clothes or mending socks or feeding the chickens.

After lunch, Zack went out on the porch to look for the turkey. And there it was, standing in the yard, just waiting for him. It seemed to know that Zack wanted to get to the machine shack, because it strutted back and forth at the bottom of the steps, a low gobble coming from its throat. Now and then it stopped, one foot off the ground, and stared at Zack sideways, with one dark, beady eye.

"You just wait," Zack said. "When I finish my trouble-shooter, you big fat bunch of trouble, you'll be sorry you ever pecked me."

But Tailpipe seemed to have all the time in the world to wait. He would move off toward the evergreen grove in one direction or the garden in the other, but the minute Zack started down the steps, back he flew, wings spread, and Zack would run up on the porch again.

Okay, Zack thought. *I can play the waiting game too.*

Finally the turkey went behind the lilac bush. Zack rushed down the steps and ran like the wind.

But Tailpipe had been watching all the while and started after him. It was too late, though, to catch up, and Zack yanked open the rickety door of the shack, tumbled inside, and banged it closed after him. He turned around and jumped a mile. There on the floor sat Josie, her legs crossed.

"Hi," she said. "Running a race or something?"

"Sort of," said Zack, letting out his breath and trying to look calm. "What are you doing here?"

Josie shrugged. "Just looking for something to do. What else have you got that needs fixing?"

"*You* put the wheel on my wagon?" Zack asked.

"I had a spare wheel, that's all," said Josie. "Your grandma helped." She pointed to the wagon with the screen nailed to the back and the rain gutter nailed to the screen. "What's all this?"

There was no point in lying. "I'm making a machine," Zack said.

Josie looked the wagon over. "What will it do?"

"Scare a turkey," said Zack.

"How?"

Zack picked up a croquet ball. He dropped it down the piece of rain gutter. The ball came out the other end and whammed against the front rim of the wagon.

"Oh," said Josie. Then she said, "What else do you need? Maybe I can help."

"Well," said Zack, "we could use a little more noise."

"What else?" asked Josie.

"We could use water, maybe, that would shoot out in all directions."

"What else?"

"We could use my friend Matthew, who keeps saying he's coming to the farm with me but always has an excuse."

"I'll be waiting," said Josie. "In the meantime, we've got another problem. The burglar struck again."

"Really?" Zack sat down on a box. This

was starting to get interesting. "What did he take this time?"

"The key to my brother's apartment."

"Why would he do that?" Zack asked.

"Because!" Josie gave him a look that meant, *Don't you get it?* "Once he has the key to a house or an apartment, he doesn't even have to climb in through a window. He can just wait till everyone's gone, then walk right up to the door and let himself in."

That almost seemed too easy. "When did Adam find out it was missing?"

"Last week. He had our truck loaded up with stuff from his room, and when he got to the city and reached in his pocket, the key was gone," Josie told him.

"The thief took the key right out of his pocket?"

"I don't know, but Adam was really mad. He had to go to the landlord and get another key, then take it to a hardware store and make a duplicate." Josie looked down at the wagon with the screen and the rain gutter and the croquet ball. "Do you think this machine could help scare off a burglar?"

Eleven

SHOW ME

The next Saturday there were two boys in the pickup truck, one in an orange T-shirt with a race car on the front, the other in a purple T-shirt with a skull and crossbones. They'd be staying overnight at the farm, and Matthew had brought along his backpack. He was very quiet. Zack's dad was at the wheel, Matthew was over by the window, and Zack was squeezed in the middle.

But Zack was right where he wanted to be. When they reached the farm, old skull-and-crossbones Matthew would have to climb out first. And while the turkey was chasing his friend, Zack could make a run for the porch. It was about time Matthew found out how hard it was to run away from a turkey.

It wasn't long before the neat blocks of houses and trees and driveways were left behind, and the pickup truck was whizzing along a four-lane highway.

The houses were getting farther and farther apart, with long stretches of land where there were only trees and no cornfields. More stretches of land with only cornfields and no trees.

At last the truck turned onto a two-lane road that went up a little hill and down again.

It turned once more onto a gravel road. And finally, after it had passed some more farms, it turned up a narrow dirt lane straight into the clearing beside Grandpa's house.

And Tailpipe was waiting.

When the truck came to a stop, the old gobbler spread its wings and flew over, as if to peck at it.

Matthew's eyes went wide when he saw just how big the turkey really was, and Zack could feel his friend's knees shaking next to his own.

"Is that it?" Matthew whispered to Zack.

"That's him," said Zack.

Dad got out of his side of the truck and began unloading feed sacks from the back.

Matthew was still watching the turkey.

"Well," he said at last. "It's just an old bird, after all. It's not a mad dog or a charging bull or anything." He opened the passenger-side door and climbed down.

The turkey attacked. It flew at Matthew, gobbling loudly, its feet scuttling along the ground, feathers flying.

"Ouch!" Matthew yelped as the turkey pecked. *Peck, peck, peck.*

Matthew swung his arms and kicked his feet, and meanwhile Zack climbed out the other door and made it up onto the porch. This time, when Matthew followed, the turkey flew halfway up the steps behind him before it gave up the chase.

Grandpa came out just then.

"Well, well! Two boys for the price of one!" he said, and grinned. "I can always use an extra farmhand around here." He went to help Dad unload the feed sacks, as Zack and Matthew went inside.

"Man! That turkey sure can peck!" said Matthew, rubbing his leg. "I can't wait to see *him* go flying!"

"*Told* you!" said Zack.

Grandma had breakfast on the table and smiled when she saw Zack's friend.

"This is Matthew. He lives down the street from us," Zack said.

"Glad to have you, Matthew, and you're

just in time," she said as she placed a platter of waffles on the table. "Ham and eggs coming up. I hope you're both hungry."

"I'm always hungry," said Matthew, and dug his fork into the waffle on top.

When breakfast was over, Zack asked Matthew to help with some chores. They carried two piles of old magazines up to the attic, brought down a fan for the kitchen, crawled under the sink to plug a hole around a pipe, and checked the mousetraps in the closets. Matthew was glad to see they were empty.

When the work was done, the boys went outside and looked for Tailpipe. The turkey was at the far end of Grandma's garden. They saw Josie sitting on top of the woodpile next to the machine shack. She scrambled down when she saw them coming.

"Josie, this is Matthew," Zack said, and turning to Matthew, "Josie's the one who put a new wheel on the wagon."

"Hi, Matthew," said Josie.

Matthew didn't even answer. He just unwrapped a stick of gum, stuck it in his mouth, and said to Zack, "I thought it was just you and me."

"Nope," said Zack. "It's the three of us."

Matthew shrugged. "So let's see the trouble-shooter machine," he said.

The three went inside the shack.

Zack could tell right away that Matthew didn't think much of what he'd made so far.

"We can pull it wherever we need it to go," Zack explained. "And it makes a really loud bang to begin with." To demonstrate, he picked up a croquet ball and dropped it down the rain gutter. It rolled out the bottom and hit the front end of the wagon with a bang.

Matthew went on chewing his gum. "You could just pick up a croquet ball and throw it at the wagon, and it would make the same noise," he said.

Zack knew that, but he was only getting started. Matthew may have been the first friend he had made when the family moved to their new house, but he wasn't always such a *great* friend. And right now he wasn't much fun, and he certainly wasn't being very polite to Josie.

"Well . . . there's a lot more to do," Zack explained.

"Yeah," said Josie, looking Matthew square in the face. "This is only step number one. You've only seen the beginning of the turkey trouble-shooter."

"Okay," said Matthew, "so show me!"

87

Twelve

Twelve

MOVING DAY

Zack was thinking so hard and so fast his brain hurt. The problem was that he had already tried all kinds of things with the wagon and the lazy Susan, and none of them had worked out. All week he had been going over ideas of what he would try next. He wasn't sure of anything, but he had to say *something*.

"Next," he said, reaching into his pocket and pulling out a pack of balloons left over from Emilene's birthday party, "we need some water balloons," and he handed one to Matthew, another to Josie. "You can fill them at the pump on the back porch."

While Matthew and Josie were up at the house, Zack went digging desperately through the stuff on his grandpa's workbench, looking for the lightweight pie tin he had seen before. He drove a thin, sharp nail through the center of it so that it stuck out the other side.

When his friends came back, he showed them the nail in the pie tin. "We need to arrange things so that the pie tin is standing up on edge with a water balloon behind it. When the ball shoots out the end of the rain gutter, it will hit the pie tin, which will fall backward onto the balloon; the nail will pop it, and there will be this big bang, with water all over the place."

Now Matthew began to look a little bit interested. He took the gum out of his mouth, and stuck it to the floor of the wagon a few inches from the end of the rain gutter. He stuck the edge of the pie tin in the gum so that it was standing straight up. Then Josie placed her water balloon between the back of the pie tin and the rim of the wagon.

"Ready?" said Zack.

"Go!" Matthew and Josie said together.

Zack dropped the croquet ball down the top of the piece of rain gutter. It rolled out the other end and hit the pie tin, but only hard enough to tip it slightly, not knock it over.

This time Matthew didn't make fun of it. He only said, "I think the rain gutter should be longer."

"You're right," said Zack, and now his brain was in overdrive. "We need to start higher. A lot higher. Because when the water balloon bursts, that's only the beginning."

Josie was looking at him curiously, but

Zack barreled on: "We have to build it some-place where it can stay awhile."

"Yeah!" said Josie, watching him all the while. "If you can't take the machine to the turkey, we'll get the turkey to come to the machine."

Zack couldn't have said it better himself.

"Right. So I think we should build it in the barn," Zack continued. "Grandpa doesn't use it much in summer. And we can haul our stuff there on the wagon. Now we just have to figure out what to take."

Matthew was already moving slowly around the shack, shaking cans to guess what was inside and opening boxes. Josie, too, started checking out barrels and climb-ing on cinder blocks to see what was up on the shelves.

"Man, this place is a museum!" Matthew said. "Bird feeders, an old sewing machine. Some kind of propeller."

Josie even found a can of marbles. "Your grandma uses these to spread around plants in her window garden," she said.

"And look at this!" said Zack. He held up a toy gum-ball machine, with one red faded-looking candy rattling around inside. There was a lid at the top to add more gum balls and a trapdoor at the bottom to let them out. "I'll bet this was my dad's when he was a kid."

Matthew found a fireplace bellows too. When you moved the handles out and in, it squeezed out puffs of air. Matthew pointed the nozzle at the back of Josie's head and pumped the bellows. Josie's hair stuck straight up in the air.

The first thing to do was make the rain gutter longer. So Zack and Matthew picked up all the sections of rain pipe they could find and put them on the wagon. They kept piling on stuff—the washing machine

wringer, a steering wheel, and a bicycle pump; the bellows, the marbles, a roasting pan, and the propeller. They even added the gum-ball machine.

When they couldn't fit one more thing on the wagon, they opened the door of the shack and looked out—Zack one way, and Matthew the other.

"What are you waiting for?" asked Josie, who was at the back of the wagon, trying to hold the load together.

"The turkey's standing right out by the silo," said Zack, "and he's looking our way."

"So?" said Josie.

"So the minute we step out there pulling this creaky wagon, he's going to peck us up one side and down the other, that's what," said Matthew.

"He never pecks me," said Josie.

The boys turned around and stared at her.

"Why not? 'Cause you're a *girl*?" Matthew

asked. "'Cause he's too polite to peck a girl?"

Josie rolled her eyes. "Watch," she said, and motioned for Matthew to hold on to the load in the wagon. Then she squeezed between the two boys in the doorway.

In fact, she walked right out into the open space between the barn and the machine shack. When Tailpipe saw her, he spread his wings and began to gobble. But as he came skittering across the ground, head down and feathers flying, Josie reached one hand into the pocket of her jeans, pulled out a handful of Cheerios, and threw them directly in the path of the turkey.

Just like magic, the turkey's whirling feet began to slow, the wings began to fold, and then he called to the hens and began to *peck, peck* at the Cheerios.

"Works every time," said Josie.

The boys stared at the turkey. They stared

at each other. Why hadn't *they* thought of that?

"Well," said Matthew, after a moment, "so we'll build a turkey-scaring machine anyway, for the times it *doesn't* work."

"It's got to do more than scare a turkey," said Josie. She looked at Zack. "Have you told him?"

"Told me what?" asked Matthew.

"Wait till we get inside the barn," said Josie.

Matthew pulled the wagon, Zack walked along one side to steady the load, and Josie followed behind to see that nothing fell off. When they got inside, Matthew looked all around, his eyes huge. Zack wondered if he'd ever been inside a real barn before.

"Now," Matthew said. "Tell me what?"

But first Josie had a few questions. She looked hard at Matthew and asked, "What do you know about detective work?"

Matthew looked from Josie to Zack and shrugged.

"Have you ever had a break-in at your house?" Josie asked.

"No," said Matthew.

"Has anyone ever broken into your dad's car?"

"No," said Matthew.

"Has anyone ever stolen anything from your backpack?"

"No," said Matthew.

Josie sighed and looked at Zack. "Maybe he can help and maybe he can't," she said.

"Josie thinks there's a burglar robbing the farms around here," said Zack. "A really clever burglar."

"Thinks? *Knows!*" said Josie. "The Smiths' snowblower, the Baileys' angel food cake, the Hendersons' pig, my mom's gold bracelet, Zack's grandma's earring, my brother's key to his apartment . . ."

"Wow!" said Matthew. "Anybody get fingerprints? Any clues?"

"All we found were some sneaker prints in the ground outside one of our windows where he probably crawled in," said Josie. "V marks, like a duck makes."

"So maybe it was a duck," said Matthew, but no one laughed.

"Well, the only thing we can do right this minute is work on that machine," Zack said. Now that he'd *finally* gotten Matthew to the farm, he didn't want to waste time. Especially if a burglar was coming back.

Thirteen

DOWN THE RAIN GUTTER

The largest part of Grandpa's barn, with the rafters above and the stack of hay in one corner, was at the very front, the part of the barn a person would see first when he walked through the big double doors. The stalls for the cows were farther back, with a door that opened to the pasture.

All sorts of things hung from nails—a raincoat, a harness, a cap, a rope. An old pegboard leaned crookedly against the wall, where it had fallen among the cobwebs.

Zack and his friends took over the large

space and went through the pile of junk they had brought from the machine shack, trying out first one thing, then another, to see what could work. After they had fitted sections of rain gutter together, they brought the stepladder from the back porch and nailed one end of the gutter up high on one of the thick posts that held up the roof. Josie could drop the croquet ball down it by standing on the next-to-the-last step of the ladder and holding on to the post.

When the dinner bell rang at lunchtime, they didn't really want to stop. But they washed their hands at the pump and headed into the kitchen, where the grown-ups were already eating.

"You three young'uns have been mighty busy," Grandpa said as he helped himself to the chicken and noodles.

"What's all that pounding and rattling going on in the barn?" asked Zack's dad.

"We're working on a machine," said Zack.

"What kind of a machine is that?" asked Grandma.

"We'll show you when we're done," said Josie.

"Can we keep it there in the barn while we're working on it?" Zack asked.

"You can keep it there for the summer, but once cold weather sets in, we'll be parking our car in there at night," Grandpa said. "And while you're working around out there, keep an eye out for a gold watch chain, because mine has disappeared."

"Oh, Ned! Did you lose that?" said Grandma.

Zack and Josie looked at each other.

"What's a watch chain?" asked Matthew, taking another roll from the bread basket the minute he'd finished his first one.

"Oh, Zack's granddaddy likes old-timey things, and it used to belong to *his* own father,"

Grandma explained. "Back then men had round watches that slipped into a pocket and were attached by a little chain. Ned always carried his around in his overalls."

"Then the chain came off the watch, and the next thing I knew, it was gone. Probably lost it somewhere out in the field," said Grandpa.

"Just like my silver earring." Grandma sighed. "The little things you like the most are the ones that disappear."

When Zack and Matthew and Josie went back to the barn, all Josie wanted to talk about was the burglar.

"That's two things stolen from your grandparents' house, Zack, and two things stolen from mine!" she exclaimed. "I thought maybe the burglar just took one thing from every house and moved on, but I guess not. He's back, and he'll probably come again."

"Do you suppose he comes at night?" Zack asked.

"He's got to!" said Josie. "If he came during the day, someone would see him. Mom's almost always home unless she comes over here to visit. It would be hard to miss a stranger walking around a farmyard."

"When do you think the machine will be ready to fire?" asked Matthew.

"I'm not sure. We've still got a lot of work to do," Zack told him.

"Then can I come again next week?" Matthew asked.

"Sure, if you're not too scared of the turkey," Zack teased.

When Matthew pulled out his package of gum again, he offered a stick to both Josie and Zack.

Now that the top of the long rain gutter was high on a post, the problem was what to do with the other end of it. Zack knew he could set the pie tin and water balloon on the barn floor, of course, but once the ball reached the ground, the show was over. They needed things to happen at different levels all the way down, so he and his friends went back to the machine shack to look for something as high as their heads.

The only thing they could find was a skinny six-drawer dresser, warped by rain, with a broken foot that made it lean to one side. There wasn't much in the drawers—just a couple of coat hangers and some old paint-stained shirts belonging to Gramps. The boys took out all the drawers so they could carry it more easily, and with Matthew and Josie holding one end and Zack holding the other, they got it inside the barn and standing at the end of the dangling rain gutter.

Matthew was still panting. "Now what?" he asked.

"Now we figure out a way to set up the pie tin and water balloon on top of the dresser," Zack told him.

This wasn't too difficult. Once again, Matthew took the gum out of his mouth and used it to hold the pie tin in place. Zack donated his gum to keep the balloon from bobbing away.

Josie was already climbing the step-ladder. "Can we try it?" she asked.

"Fire away," said Zack.

Rattle, rattle, rattle went the ball as it fell through one section of rain gutter, then the next and the next. On the dresser top, it shot out the curved end of the rain gutter, slammed into the pie tin, and the next thing they knew, there was a loud *SPLOPP!* as the balloon burst, water sprayed all over the place, and the ball dropped down onto the dirt floor.

The three kids cheered.

"Not bad for a first try!" said Zack, giving Matthew and Josie high fives.

Maybe they wouldn't be able to point their machine in any direction they wanted, but this was a start.

Fourteen

MATTHEW AT NIGHT

"**N**ow we need something about as high as our shoulders for the next level," said Zack. He and Matthew went back to the machine shack while Josie headed to the porch to fill another water balloon.

All the while, Zack's hand was in his pocket, around a fistful of rice puffs he had taken from a cereal box in the kitchen. This time he was prepared for Tailpipe when he attacked. But of course this time the turkey was nowhere in sight.

There was an old three-drawer file

cabinet in one dark corner of the shack, half-covered with a canvas tarp. Josie came back in time to help them open the rusty drawers.

"Magazines!" she said. "There must be a hundred *National Geographics* in there."

Armload by armload, they took out all the magazines and stacked them in the empty dresser drawers that were sitting about. Then they managed to tip the empty file cabinet onto the wagon and pull it back to the barn. They set it up at the place the croquet ball would probably land when it rolled off the top of the dresser.

"Now what?" asked Josie, turning to Zack.

But Zack was already looking through their junk pile, and he picked up a dented rectangular cake pan. He set it on the file cabinet, half on, half off, and his friends knew right away what he was thinking.

"I'll drop the ball this time," said Matthew, with a grin, and he climbed to the top of the stepladder and plunked the croquet ball down the rain gutter.

Rattle, rattle, rattle it went again, with another loud *SPLOPP!* as the second water balloon burst, and then a *BANG!* as the ball rolled off the leaning dresser top, hit the part of the pan that hung over the edge of the file cabinet, and sent both pan and ball to the ground.

"Wow!" cried Zack. Their second success of the day!

"Boy genius!" Matthew said, slapping him on the back. "Way to go!"

The only thing they could find in the shack that was waist high was the old treadle sewing machine. It didn't run by electricity, but by a person moving the big wide pedal up and down with her feet.

It was too heavy to carry far, so—just

as they had done with the file cabinet—the boys tipped it over onto the wagon and pulled it to the barn. Zack didn't know yet what they would do with a sewing machine, but he figured they had done pretty well for their first day of working together. Now they were getting tired, and Josie had to go home.

"Next Saturday then?" she asked. "We'll think about something the ball can do next?"

"Yeah, something that makes a *huge* noise," said Matthew.

"I'll work on it," said Zack.

When Zack and his dad stayed overnight at the farm, they slept in the two small bedrooms at the top of the stairs. The roof slanted down, so that in both bedrooms, the ceiling was high on one side of the room and low on the other.

Zack and Matthew took the bedroom

with the twin beds. Because Matthew was the guest, Zack let him sleep in the bed on the high ceiling side so he wouldn't bump his head if he sat up quickly during the night. Zack got into his bed first and told Matthew to turn out the light when he was ready.

But Matthew just sat on the edge of his bed in his Spider-Man pajamas and looked around. First he said his leg itched. Then he said he wanted to read awhile, maybe, and then he was too warm.

The next time Zack looked over, Matthew was holding something in his hands. Something wrapped up in a pair of underwear.

"Uh . . . Zack?" Matthew said. "Can I tell you something?"

"Okay," said Zack.

"I sort of have to have a night-light on when I sleep. That all right with you?"

Zack tried to think what a night-light

was. He seemed to remember a teddy bear night-light when he was three.

"Sure. Whatever," Zack said.

"Thanks." Matthew unfolded the underwear and took out a little football night-light. He plugged it in the wall socket, then turned off the ceiling light. The small football glowed orange in the dark room.

"Good night," said Zack.

"You won't tell anyone, will you?" said Matthew. "Promise you won't tell Josie."

"I promise," Zack said.

It had been a busy day, and Zack was really tired. He felt himself falling asleep almost as soon as he rolled over, the pillow soft against his cheek.

He didn't know how long he had slept, but suddenly he heard the floor creak, then creak again. And then he imagined that someone was standing beside his bed, looking down at him in the dark.

Fifteen

IN THE MOONLIGHT

Zack opened one eye, then the other. Somebody *was* standing beside his bed. It was Matthew.

"Zack!" his friend whispered, tugging at his arm. "I see something."

"What?" Zack asked, but Matthew crawled toward the window.

"Come here and look!" he said.

Zack swung his legs over the side of the bed and crouched down beside him. In the moonlight, they could just make out a pickup truck moving slowly up the lane with its lights off.

"I was just sitting here, looking out the window, when I saw this truck coming down the road out there," Matthew whispered. "I watched it slow down when it got near your grandpa's place, and then its lights went off and it started up the lane!"

"What time is it?" Zack asked, wide awake now.

"Twelve thirty. I couldn't get to sleep," Matthew said.

"Why would somebody turn off his lights before he parked?" Zack wondered aloud. "And who would be coming here in the middle of the night?"

"Exactly!" said Matthew. "Only one person: a robber. He doesn't want his headlights flashing on anyone's wall."

Goose bumps broke out on Zack's arms. Always before, he had only half believed Josie's stories about a burglary, but now . . .

Was it possible that he and Matthew could catch the burglar?

"Who owns a pickup truck around here?" asked Matthew.

"Everybody!" said Zack. "The Smiths, the Baileys, the Hendersons, the Wellses, the Morenos . . ."

The pickup crept into the clearing between the house and barn, turned around, and stopped. Nothing happened for a few seconds. It was too dark to see anything clearly, but the moonlight helped. Zack kept his eyes focused on the truck.

Finally he saw the driver's door open, and a figure in dark pants and a hoodie sweatshirt stepped out. If the turkey figured he owned the place like Grandma said, and was trying to take the place of their old dog Trixie, where was he now that they needed him? Zack thought.

The person in the hooded sweatshirt

slowly swung the door of the barn wide open without a sound and went inside.

"Oh, man!" Zack said, scrambling to his feet. "If only our machine was ready to go! Let's get out there!"

Matthew grabbed his arm. "We'd better wake your dad!"

"There isn't time! All we need is the license number to give to the police and they'll arrest him. Come *on*!"

At that moment the hooded figure came back out. He was carrying something big in his arms and was heading toward his truck.

"*Hurry!*" Zack said, pulling Matthew up from the floor.

The boys softly opened the door of their room and tiptoed across the hall and down the stairs. They went out the back door without turning on a single light.

By now the intruder was climbing back

116

into the truck. This time, the engine didn't even turn on. The thief must have simply released the brake, for the pickup began rolling slowly down the sloping lane toward the road.

The boys ran after it barefoot, as close as they dared—staying on the grass rather than the lane for fear the driver would see them in the rearview mirror. But because the truck's lights weren't on, neither was the light on the license plate.

"I can't see it!" Matthew whispered hoarsely. "It's too dark!"

"It's getting away!" cried Zack.

Just as the pickup turned onto the main road, the engine started, the lights came on, and the boys scrambled up the bank, trying hard to read the license number as the truck sped away. Zack could make out the letters *XPA* and maybe the number five, but he wasn't sure.

"What was it?" he asked, turning to Matthew. "Did you see it?"

"*X* something. *XP*? I didn't get any numbers at all, did you?"

"I think it was *XPA* and maybe a five, but I couldn't see the rest. Dang it!" Zack cried. "Now we know for sure there's a robber, but we don't even know what he took!"

He let out his breath and punched himself on the arm. "You were right. I should have tried to wake up Dad, but he wouldn't have got out here in time." Zack rubbed one bare foot where he'd stepped on a stone. A prickly weed was stuck to his pajama leg, and he pulled it off before starting back to the house.

"Well, if his license plate did begin with *XPA* and a five, that's a start," said Matthew.

But Zack was miserable. "Who knows what the guy took? Next time he could load up a cow, driving up in the dark like that!"

119

"Next time we'll be ready!" said Matthew.

But it was hard for Zack to sleep after that. Did Matthew really think that the robber only came on weekends? That he'd only come when the boys were there? That he'd even come back at all. How could they tell Josie that they had actually *seen* the burglar drive up to the barn, load something into his truck, and drive off without even trying to stop him? Without even waking his dad?

"Arrrggghhh!" Zack moaned, and turned his face to the wall.

Sixteen

XPA 5

"You boys are unusually quiet," Grandma said at breakfast.

"Must have worn themselves out yesterday," Zack's dad said as he handed Matthew a plate of bacon. "We've got to leave early today, boys, after I help Gramps do a few things. Got some work to do at home."

"I'm going to send along some of my cinnamon rolls for your mom and Emilene," Grandma told Zack. She winked. "And I tucked in a few extra for you and Matthew."

Zack managed a smile. He was almost

glad they were leaving. He didn't want to face Josie after what had happened. He hung around the table after breakfast in case Dad and Gramps might talk about anything they'd found missing. But Grandpa had milked the cows, then he and Zack's dad had replaced some shingles on the roof. If something big had been taken from the barn, Zack thought, surely it would have been discovered missing by now.

He and Matthew checked on their machine, of course, but everything was there, just as they had left it. So they did some chores for Grandma, and then it was time to go.

"Good-bye, Gram. See you next week," Zack said.

"I'm coming too, if it's okay," said Matthew.

"Of course," said Grandma. "Long as you two boys don't get into mischief, you're welcome to come along."

Zack's mind was on the burglar, not the turkey, and both boys got pecked as they climbed into the truck, Tailpipe almost climbing in after them. *Next* time, Zack told himself as he slammed the truck door, he'd be armed with Cheerios when he came to Grandpa's. Every time he forgot, it seemed, he got pecked. When he was watching for the gobbler, the old tom was somewhere else.

"Dad," he said as they drove along the highway, "how many cars have the same three letters on their license plates?"

"No idea," said Dad. "Thousands? There are different license plates for each state, you know."

"How about the same three letters of the alphabet and the same next number? Like . . . oh . . . *XPA* five or something?" asked Matthew.

Dad shook his head. "You'd have to ask someone else. I'm not an expert on license plates. Why?"

123

"Just wondering," said Zack. "I mean, if somebody saw an accident and remembered only a few of the letters or numbers, would it help or not?"

"I suppose anything at all might help. Narrow it down a little, anyway. That's one reason I keep a pencil there in my glove compartment. I wouldn't trust my memory to remember a license plate if I saw an accident, so I'd write it down."

It was a pretty awful week. Zack felt sure that any day his grandmother would call and say, "Zack, tell your father that we discovered our lawn mower is missing," or "Zack, do you have any idea where our wheelbarrow could be?"

"What makes *you* so moody?" Emilene asked him when she found him out on the back steps, his head buried in his arms.

"Just thinking," said Zack, and raised his head.

"About what?" said Emilene.

"About going to jail," said Zack. "I know that a person could go to jail if he helped rob a bank, but if he just *saw* someone rob a bank and didn't say anything, do you suppose they could put him in jail for that?"

"No," said Emilene, "because if he didn't say anything, nobody would ever know. Right?" And then she said, "If I make a banana split, will you eat half?"

It was the nicest thing Emilene had said to him all week, so Zack said yes. And he really did feel better when he scooped up a spoonful of chocolate syrup and butterscotch together and put it in his mouth.

But then Emilene said, "*You* didn't see anyone rob a bank, did you?"

"No, but what if I did?"

"Then you should tell the police and they'd want you to come to court and you'd have to describe the robber and what kind of car he was driving and the color of his shirt and everything."

"What if you didn't know any of that?" asked Zack. "What if it was so dark you couldn't tell?"

"Then you might as well stay home," said Emilene, and she got up to put more strawberries on her ice cream.

When Matthew came over with his catcher's mitt and ball and wanted Zack to toss him a few, Zack said no.

"I don't think I'll ever want to play catch again if that robber stole something important from Grandma and Gramps," he said.

"Well, not playing catch with me won't help," said Matthew.

That was true. But Matthew wanted to solve the case themselves as much as Zack did, and even though they threw the ball back and forth for a while, they didn't have their hearts in it.

◆ ◆ ◆

That Friday after Dad came home from work, he got into the pickup truck with Zack and Matthew and their backpacks, and off they went again.

This time Zack remembered to put Cheerios in his pocket, but when he and Matthew climbed out and didn't see the turkey, they started on toward the house. Tailpipe saw them, however. He came around from behind, and by the time Zack heard the flap of his wings, it was too late, and he felt the familiar *peck, peck, peck* on his legs. Tailpipe got Matthew, too.

"We're going to finish that machine this weekend for sure," said Matthew. "That old turkey's pecked me for the last time."

The boys checked the barn, and as far as they could tell, all their stuff was right where they had left it, scattered about the barn floor. The wheelbarrow, the lawn mower, and the stepladder were just where they'd always been too, so the burglar hadn't taken those.

The barn was dark, though, and rain began to fall. So after dinner, the boys decided to stay indoors and play video games, then work on their trouble-shooter the next day.

They had just helped Grandma clear the table when Josie's brother tapped on the back door and stepped inside.

"Mom sent these paper plates and napkins over for your celebration tomorrow," he called to Gram from the doorway. "She thought you might want to have them before the other folks get here."

Zack realized too late that tomorrow was his grandmother's birthday and he had not gotten her a present. Could anything else go wrong?

"Why, I'll be glad to have them," Grandma

said. "But you have to come in here and eat a piece of my blueberry pie."

"Talked me into it, but I've got to take off these wet shoes," said Adam. He slipped off his sneakers and padded in his stocking feet over to the table, where Grandpa and Dad were finishing their coffee and pie.

"How you doin', Zack?" Adam said. And then to Dad, "How are things with you?"

Zack pulled Matthew out on the back porch to tell him that tomorrow was Grandma's birthday, and they'd have to think of something to give her. But then his eyes suddenly fell on the wet footprints Adam's shoes had made on the porch. Four big footprints, with tread marks in the shape of a V.

Zack froze. He looked through the kitchen doorway at Adam eating pie at the table. Then he looked at Adam's pickup truck in the clearing.

Was it possible . . . ?

"C'mon," he said to Matthew. "Pull a raincoat over your head."

Matthew gave him a quizzical look as Zack lifted two old raincoats off the hooks along the wall and noiselessly opened the back screen door.

"*What?*" Matthew kept saying, as they made their way across the wet grass.

Zack walked around the back of the truck, holding the raincoat over his head, and pointed to the license plate. And there, plain as day, it read, *XPA 5820.*

Seventeen

TESTING, TESTING . . .

Upstairs, where the grown-ups couldn't hear them, Zack and Matthew sat across from each other on the twin beds, faces turned toward the window. Outside the rain pattered down on the roof, and pretty soon they heard Adam saying good-bye to Grandma and Grandpa, and from the window, they watched him jump into the pickup truck.

"How are we going to tell Josie that her own brother is the thief?" Zack said. "Everything figures. All the burglaries started happening after Adam got home from the navy."

"Maybe he just got mixed up with the wrong crowd," Matthew suggested. "But I still don't get it. If Josie told you that the thief had V-shaped treads on his shoes, and those were his sneaker prints outside the window of his own house, why did he have to climb in a window to steal his mom's bracelet? He could have walked right in through the door."

"Because he *wanted* it to look as though a burglar had been there and climbed through the window, once she discovered her bracelet missing," said Zack.

"Then he should have thrown away his sneakers," said Matthew. "That's evidence, plain as day."

They sat silently a few minutes more, trying to figure it all out.

"Who do you suppose he's selling all this

stuff to in town?" asked Zack. "Maybe he's not going to start college at all. Maybe he just rented an apartment so he could store all the stuff he's stealing. Though he's probably eaten the angel food cake he stole by now."

"So he's got a pig and a snowblower in the apartment too?" asked Matthew, pulling his feet up on the bed and sitting cross-legged.

"I just don't know," said Zack. He took a deep breath, held it a moment, and let it out. But whoever left the V-shaped tread marks outside the window, Josie had said, was a heavy man with big feet, which fit her brother exactly. As for bothering to steal an angel food cake, hadn't Grandma said a few weeks ago that when Adam was sixteen, he'd eaten half a dozen of her biscuits, one right after the other?

"Well," said Matthew finally. "Are we going to finish making that machine tomorrow or not?"

"I suppose," said Zack. "But it's Grandma's birthday and I didn't even get anything for her."

"Sometimes my mom says the best present I can give her is to keep out of her way," Matthew told him.

"We'll see," said Zack, just as a streak of lightning lit up the sky.

Matthew covered his head with his arms and dived under the covers as a clap of thunder shook the room.

As though to make up for the storm of the night before, Saturday morning was beautiful. Every drop of rain clinging to the leaves sparkled in the bright sunlight, and when Zack and Matthew came down to breakfast, Josie was there at the table.

"All ready to go to work?" she asked eagerly, her mouth half-full of sausage.

Zack knew right away that this wouldn't

be the time to tell her about her brother.

"Sure," he said.

"Well, today's Grandma's birthday, Zack," his dad said from his side of the table. "Your mother and Emilene are coming this afternoon for the party, and I want you kids to be as helpful as possible."

"My family's coming too!" said Josie. "Mom said it'll be a nice celebration, because when a person reaches seventy, she—"

"Whoa! Whoa!" said Grandpa. "Never tell a woman's age."

"Oh, I don't mind a bit," said Grandma, laughing. "I never felt better. But if you kids would sweep the front porch, and keep out of my kitchen till lunchtime, that would be a blessing."

"Sure," said Zack. "And if there's anything else you want us to do, just tell us. Happy birthday, Gram!"

❖ ❖ ❖

If Adam came again in the middle of the night—on a Friday night, that is, when Zack and Matthew were here, Zack was thinking—they'd be ready. If they were awake, that is. *If* they were watching from the window. *If*, when they saw a pickup truck pull in the lane with its lights off, they could get to the barn before it reached the clearing. There were a lot of ifs.

Josie, with a polka-dot ribbon around her ponytail, was so excited about finishing the machine that she fairly jumped about the barn, and the three of them worked hard all morning. They taped the sections of the rain gutter together so they couldn't easily come apart, and filled a few more balloons with water.

Zack placed the toy gum-ball machine, filled with marbles, on top of the old sewing machine table. A string was fastened to the little knob that opened the trapdoor at the bottom to let gum balls fall out. The other end of the string was tied to the metal handle of one of the file cabinet drawers.

If everything worked as planned, the croquet ball would shoot down the long stretch of rain gutter, pop out the other end, and slam into the pie tin with the nail in it, which would fall back and pop the balloon.

As water exploded all over the place, the ball would roll off the sloping dresser and fall onto the rectangular cake pan resting half on, half off, the file cabinet below.

The cake pan with the ball in it would fall onto the string stretched tight between the file cabinet and gum-ball machine, and all the marbles would fall out with an awful racket into a tin bucket there on the floor.

If everything worked as planned.

"Do you think we're ready to test it?" asked Matthew, checking to see that the pie tin was in place, stuck to the dresser top with a fresh wad of gum.

"I am!" said Josie, climbing up the step-ladder with a croquet ball in one hand.

"Okay, then. Go!" said Zack.

Josie dropped the ball into the open end of the rain gutter. *Rattle, rattle, rattle* it went as it rolled.

Bang! it went, as it shot out the other end and hit the pie tin with the nail in it.

SPLOPP! went the water balloon as the pie tin fell over.

The ball rolled off the sloping top of the dresser, just as it had done before, but not where it was supposed to go. It missed the large rectangular cake pan and rolled a few inches on the ground before it stopped.

"Oh, man!" Matthew said, in disappointment.

Zack leaned against the post and thought. Just like a ship needing a channel, the ball needed to be guided to the place it was supposed to roll off.

"Wait here," he said. When he came back, he was carrying scissors and tape and the empty Rice Chex box he'd seen in the kitchen that morning. He cut off both ends as well as the front panel, then taped it flat onto the dresser top, the cardboard sides guiding the ball just where it needed to go. Josie put another water balloon in place.

"Let me drop the ball this time," Matthew said. He climbed the stepladder, reached as high as he could, and dropped the ball down the long sections of rain gutter. Down came the ball, bang went the pie tin, pop went the balloon, and this time the ball rolled right through the cardboard channel, went over the edge, hit the cake pan, and the pan hit the string below as it fell.

But the string hadn't been pulled tight enough, and it didn't yank open the little trapdoor of the gum-ball machine. So once again a water balloon had to be stuck behind the pie tin, the cake pan had to be placed just so, the string pulled *really* tight between the file cabinet and the gum-ball machine. And this time, everything worked.

Rattle, rattle, rattle! Bam! Pop! Bang! And finally, *finally*, the marbles tumbled with a great racket into the metal bucket below the bench. *Rat-a-tat-a-tat . . .*

"It works!" Zack yelled.

"We did it!" screamed Josie.

"Bring on the turkey!" said Matthew.

Or a robber, Zack thought.

At last, with a new water balloon in place, they were ready for the real thing. All Zack had to do was find the turkey. Get Tailpipe to chase him. It was the strangest feeling to actually *want* to hear him flapping his wings, to see him coming at Zack, feathers flying, on his whirling feet, and follow him . . . ha! Right into a trap!

Eighteen

PICTURE TIME

Grandma rang the dinner bell for lunch before they could do anything more, however, and this time the three of them beat Zack's dad and Grandpa to the table.

Dad and Gramps were still talking business.

"We've got to make sure we mend the fence in the cow pasture before summer's over," Dad said, as he made himself a sandwich from the plate of bologna and cheese. "Don't want to be out there stretching that wire with snow coming down the back of my neck."

"Good idea," said Gramps. "Last winter the snow was so deep it covered the tops of the fence posts."

"Did the Smiths ever get another snow-blower?" Zack asked.

Grandma looked up. "Why would they get another? They only need one."

Grandpa chuckled. "They forgot they had let their neighbors borrow it last year, though, and George Kemp found he still had it in his garage."

Zack looked at Josie across the table. She had stopped chewing altogether.

"You mean nobody stole it?" she asked.

"Goodness, no! Who would steal a snow-blower?" asked Gramps.

"What about the Hendersons' pig?" Josie asked.

"What about it?" asked Gramps. "They've got a lot of pigs."

"The one that was stolen! Did they ever

find the person who took it?" Josie asked, her voice rising.

"Stole a pig?" said Grandpa, and both of Zack's grandparents were looking at her now. "Where did you get that idea, Josie? That pig squeezed through a fence, got out in the pasture, and was two farms away before somebody found it. Which is another good reason to get *our* fence repaired pretty soon."

Zack decided not to say anything about an angel food cake. When he looked across at Josie this time, he could tell by the slump of her shoulders that this was not what she wanted to hear. And he was sure of it when they walked back to the barn after lunch, because she said, in a small voice, "If there wasn't a burglar, then it probably means that nobody stole my mom's gold bracelet, either. And if nobody stole it, then it *was* probably me who lost it, because I was wearing it last. I think."

145

Zack and Matthew exchanged looks.

"I don't know, Josie. There could still be a burglar around," Zack said. "Let's think about it later. Right now I'd like to find the turkey and see if the machine scares him. I think we could use a bigger water balloon than we've got there now, though. I've got a few left."

What Zack was thinking about, however, was Josie's brother and XPA 5. Maybe Adam hadn't stolen the snowblower or the pig, but he had certainly taken something from Grandma and Grandpa's barn. If Zack didn't tell Josie soon about her brother, people would start arriving for the birthday celebration. But this didn't seem like a good time to tell her either. Already he could hear the slam of a car door in the clearing, and Emilene's voice squealing out birthday greetings to Grandma. If Zack didn't tell Josie before the party was over and she went home, Adam would go right on stealing stuff in his pickup truck and taking it to sell in town. Perhaps this very night!

"Zack!" came his mother's voice. "Come and get in the picture. We're taking a family photo while everyone still looks dressed up."

"Go ahead," said Matthew. "We'll wait right here. But as soon as they take the picture, get the turkey to chase you over here so we can try out the machine for real. We'll be waiting."

Zack walked across the clearing to the lawn where the family had gathered. He was glad he didn't see the turkey now, because that would be really embarrassing if it attacked him in front of the camera.

Grandma was smiling at him. She had one arm around Emilene and the other outstretched for him.

"Come stand by me, Zack," she called. "I want my two wonderful grandchildren beside me in the picture. Oh, if I just had my silver earrings. I don't feel completely dressed without them."

Zack stood next to his grandmother and faced the camera. He absolutely hated having his picture taken. He always looked like a dork. Mr. Wells was taking the picture, and he said what photographers always say before they snap it: "Okay, now, everybody smile and say *cheese*." When everyone said 'cheese,' Zack thought, it looked like they were having their teeth cleaned at the dentist's. Their smiles were as phony as a candy cigar.

Click, went the camera.

"Now another," said Josie's dad. "This is a special day, and we want a special picture of our lovely neighbor."

At that very second, Zack saw Tailpipe strutting by. He was not looking for boys to peck, however. He was not even pecking at all. He was holding something shiny and silver in his beak and was moving quite rapidly toward the barn.

All Zack could think of was his grandma's silver earring. He broke away from the family group and started to chase the turkey.

"Zack!" Grandma cried in surprise.

"*Zack!*" yelled his dad.

"We're not done taking pictures!" called his mother.

But all Zack could say was "Gram's earring! The turkey's got it!" and then Grandma and everyone else began to follow.

Faster and faster the gobbler went, as though he knew he was being chased. The barn doors were wide open, and Josie and Matthew, who had been watching from the doorway, ducked back inside to take their places at the machine. This wasn't quite the way they had planned it—Zack chasing the turkey instead of the turkey chasing him—but they were ready.

Nineteen

THE TURKEY-BLASTER TROUBLE-SHOOTER

Just as Tailpipe came through the door-way with Zack and the others close behind, the croquet ball went whizzing down the rain gutter and out the other end, faster than it had ever gone before.

Bam! The ball crashed against the pie tin with the nail in it.

POP! The pie tin fell over and popped the balloon with an extra loud *SPLOPP!* and *WHOOSH* went the water, splashing them all.

The startled turkey rose several inches

off the ground and dropped the shiny thing in its mouth, which wasn't Grandma's earring at all—just a shiny piece of foil from one of Matthew's gum wrappers, just as . . .

BANG! went the ball as it hit the cake pan. The pan instantly fell off the edge of the file cabinet, hit the taut string tied to the trapdoor of the gum-ball machine, and almost immediately there came the *rat-a-tat-a-tat* of marbles cascading down into the tin bucket. Tailpipe whirled around in confusion.

But the turkey-blaster trouble-shooter hadn't finished. Instead of rolling onto the ground beside the sewing machine stand, the ball went right between two of its legs and dropped onto the wide pedal beneath, right where Matthew was standing.

It balanced strangely on the low end of the treadle, and—faster than a pig could squeal—Matthew did what any nine-year-old boy would do in such a situation: he stomped down on the high side of the pedal, as though it were a seesaw, as hard as he could, and lobbed the croquet ball straight up in the air like a rocket.

BAM! it went as it hit a wood rafter beneath the roof. Tailpipe jumped again.

PONG! went the ball as it ricocheted against the tall metal ladder along one wall. Tailpipe flapped his wings in panic.

WHACK! went the ball as it dropped onto a wood railing, and then . . .

PLINK! as it bounced onto a shiny milk can, then rolled off to hit the dusty pegboard propped against the wall and knocked it over.

And there, right behind it, lay a little pile of glittery sparkles and spangles and silver and gold.

As Grandma gasped and bent down to stare, Tailpipe stopped his frantic gobbling, picked up the piece of foil he had been carrying, strutted over to his shiny collection, and dropped it on top of the heap.

Everyone stepped forward.

"My earring!" Grandma said, pointing.

"My gold bracelet!" said Josie's mom, reaching down to pick it up.

And yes, there was Grandpa's watch chain and all the other little trinkets that had been dropped accidentally from time to time in the yard and in the barn and in the clearing.

Grandpa gave a low whistle. "Well, I'll be a cow's moo!" he said. "I've heard of crows collecting shiny objects, but I never heard tell of a turkey."

"That's because there's no other turkey like this one in the whole county—the whole state—the entire USA!" said Grandma. "And here I thought I'd lost my earring forever."

"And *I* thought my daughter had lost my

bracelet!" said Josie's mom. "Now I remember that I wore it over here myself the week before it went missing. The clasp must have come loose as I crossed the yard."

Tailpipe was upset that people were picking through his pile of treasures, but the minute he pecked Grandma, Grandpa chased the old Tom to the top of the haystack, and the turkey gobbled from his perch under the rafters.

But Emilene was staring at the rain gutter, the pie tin, and the gum-ball machine. "How did you get it to *do* all that?" she asked her brother. "Is *this* what you've been working on here at the farm?"

Zack grinned. "Yeah, all but the sewing machine pedal. I don't think any of us knew that *that* was going to happen! Nice going, Matthew."

"Well, if you boys hadn't been building this contraption, no telling how long it would have taken any of us to find these things," said Dad. "How did you think up something like this?"

"Amazing!" said Gramps.

They were interrupted by the sound of an engine out in the clearing, and Zack saw Adam's truck pull up in front of the barn. Zack and Matthew nudged each other. How did Adam have the nerve to show up here?

"Hello, everyone!" Adam called, getting out. "Happy birthday, Grandma Harvey! I've got a little surprise for you."

He leaned over the back of the pickup truck and lifted out a chest of polished wood with brass handles at each end.

"Oh, my goodness!" cried Grandma. "My blanket chest! Why, it looks brand-new!"

"That's from Adam and me," said Grandpa, beaming. "When one of those handles came off, I told you I'd fix it, and I carried it out to the barn. Then Adam said he'd come by some night when you were asleep and take it to his place to sand and refinish. I knew we couldn't hide anything from you if we kept it here in the house."

"Why, you two sneaks!" Grandma said delightedly, and she gave first Grandpa, then Adam, a big hug. She turned to Mr. and Mrs. Wells. "Aren't you glad this young man's home from the navy? Is there anything in the world he can't do? I can't count the times he's helped me out."

"I was thinking the same thing when he washed our windows a few weeks ago," said Josie's mom proudly. "Nothing like having a strong young man about the place, even if he is living in town."

Well, Zack thought as he exchanged looks with Matthew. That was the last piece of the puzzle. Now they knew why Adam's footprints were in the flower bed outside the Wellses' window. Now he didn't even have to tell Josie that her brother wasn't a burglar, because she'd never suspected he was.

"Hey, what's all this?" Adam said, looking around at the rain gutter, the cake pan, and the sewing machine. "This looks interesting!"

"Wait a minute, and we'll show you!" Josie told her brother. She quickly replaced the water balloon, while Zack put the pie tin and the cake pan back in place, and Matthew poured all the marbles back into the trapdoor and made sure the string on the knob was stretched tight.

Everyone wanted to see it again.

"Adam, watch!" Josie said, as she climbed the ladder.

Once again the ball went down the rain gutter, and with a *bam*, a *pop*, a *splat*, a *whoosh*, a *bang*, and a *rat-a-tat-tat*, the croquet ball did what it was supposed to do, except that this time it rolled onto the floor instead of the sewing machine treadle.

"Neat!" said Adam. "I always wanted to make something like that when I was a kid. I've got a couple of springs from an old car seat I'll bet we could fit in there somehow. I'll bring them over the next time I come."

"And there's an old washboard in my cellar you children could use," said Josie's mom. "Marbles sliding down a washboard would make a terrible racket. I feel I owe you *something* for finding my gold bracelet."

"And my earring!" said Grandma. "You don't know how much I missed that."

"Well, we didn't find anything, old Tailpipe did," said Zack, looking up at the turkey who was still gobbling his string of complaints from the top of the haystack. "And guess what, Adam, we have something for you," he said.

Zack went over to the pile of glittering doodads—the tin-can lids and gum wrappers and buckles and soda bottle caps—and picked up a shiny key. "Is this the key to your apartment, maybe?"

"Heeeey!" said Adam. "What's it doing here?"

"It's our dad-gum turkey, Adam," said Grandpa. "He's apparently been picking up everything bright and shiny that he finds in the yard and dropping them behind the old Peg-Board here in the barn. I'd put him in solitary for a while, but I doubt if it would do any good."

Zack's mom was looking over the old sewing machine. "I've always wondered how people managed to sew on a machine with their feet going back and forth on a treadle," she said. And then she looked over the whole turkey-blaster machine. "You kids have imaginations as big as the state of Iowa!"

She didn't know the half of it, Zack thought, but he was glad he'd never told her their suspicions about a burglar.

Emilene was still being a pest. "Can I try out your machine, Zack?" she kept saying. "Show me what to do. Please? *Please*?"

"We're out of balloons, but I have some more in my backpack," he told her. "I'll go get them if you help Matthew fill the gumball machine again."

As the family wandered back to the lawn chairs in the yard, Zack went up to the farmhouse and got another pack of balloons. He helped himself to one of the party sandwiches on a platter there in the kitchen and headed for the barn, almost too happy to chew.

And then, straight ahead, came Tailpipe.

He still had a few pieces of hay caught in his feathers, but he was walking erect, his two stately wings half spread on either side of him, his black and red and green feathers glinting in the afternoon sun. His two beady eyes looked right into Zack's,

161

and a low *gobble, gobble* came from behind the red wattle that wagged back and forth at his throat.

Zack stopped dead still, one sneaker in the air. Tailpipe stopped, one foot off the ground. Neither of them moved.

Then, slowly, Zack crumbled the last bite of sandwich in his hand and tossed it in front of the turkey. For one brief moment, the old gobbler waited, and then the *gobble, gobble* became a sort of *cluckity-cluck* as Tailpipe's wings came down like the flaps on a plane, his tail feathers collapsed like the closing of a fan, and a few seconds later the turkey called to the hens to come join him for lunch.

Maybe he and his friends didn't need to make a machine to scare a turkey, Zack was thinking as he walked on by and entered the barn. Maybe it wouldn't be needed to scare a burglar, either. But they still had the sewing machine pedal to work into the action, and a washing-machine wringer, and what about the little propeller they'd found in Gramps's machine shack? Adam was going to bring over some springs from a car seat, and Josie's mom had an old washboard. . . . Who knew what else they would find for their absolutely amazing, one-of-a-kind contraption?

There was a lot to do yet, and the great thing about the turkey-blaster trouble-shooter was that they never had to say it was finished.

Turn the page for a sneak peek at
roxie and the hooligans at buzzard's roost

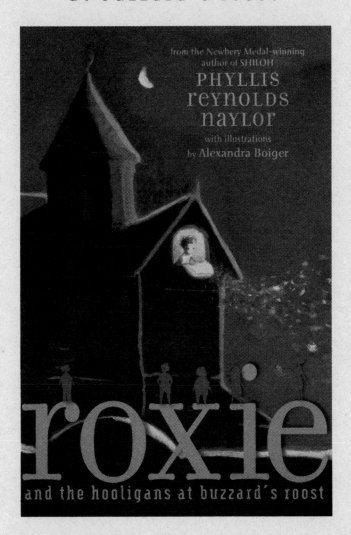

from the Newbery Medal–winning
author of SHILOH
**PHYLLIS
Reynolds
naylor**

with illustrations
by Alexandra Boiger

roxie
and the hooligans at buzzard's roost

• ON THE ROAD •

After Roxie became friends with the hooligans, they were still a troublesome lot.

Helvetia Hagus, the sturdy girl with knee socks rolled down to her ankles, would often bump another child out of line, just so she could stand next to Roxie at lunchtime.

Simon Surly would punch the nose of any boy in Public School Number Thirty-Seven who dared make fun of Roxie's big ears.

Freddy Filch would swipe a toffee candy from a classmate just to slip it into Roxie's pocket at recess.

And wiry little Smoky Jo would follow Roxie around like a shadow, telling everyone, in her squeaky voice, that she and Roxie Warbler were a team.

Because everyone along this little stretch of New England shoreline, from the town of Hasty Pudding to Hamburger-on-Bun, and even those in the village of Swiss-on-Rye, knew the story by heart: how Roxie and the hooligans had outsmarted the bank robbers, making their small village of Chin-in-Hand proud!

None of that would have happened, however, if the hooligans hadn't been perfectly dreadful to

Roxie because of her large ears, and to Norman, her best friend, just because he wore glasses. They had teased and tormented and tripped and trapped them so often that Roxie had gone to Public School Number Thirty-Seven each morning with an ache in the pit of her stomach.

And then . . . the awful day that the hooligans had chased her into a dumpster, all piling in after her, and a truck had arrived to cart it off to a barge, which was emptied far out at sea. Somehow the children had managed to swim to an island where two bank robbers were hiding. . . .

If it hadn't been for Norman back on the playground, who, even though the hooligans had knocked his glasses off, had figured out what was happening with the dumpster, there might never have been the dramatic rescue by helicopter that was talked about for many weeks.

Roxie, however, was a bit tired of all the attention, and was delighted when school was out for the summer, because Uncle Dangerfoot was taking her on vacation to a place called Buzzard's Roost to celebrate her daring adventure.

"I wish you and Daddy were coming too," Roxie said as her mother brushed her hair. Roxie's ears stuck straight out from her head like the handles on a sugar bowl, so her hair was often a tangle.

"I do too, Love, but Papa and I have to tend the shop," her mother said. "You'll come back and tell us all about it. And don't forget to take your bathing suit and sandals."

Right that very minute, Uncle Dangerfoot

drove up to the cottage in a car that pulled a small trailer. A beach umbrella stuck out one window of the trailer, and a kite bobbed from the other. Across the street, the hooligans watched, their mouths turned down at the corners.

Mrs. Warbler had tea and crumpets ready for him when Uncle Dangerfoot came up the walk. The man who had wrestled alligators and jumped from planes was not to be kept waiting, and he never began a trip without a good, bracing cup of hot tea.

He wore a jungle helmet and a tan safari jacket with brass buttons. And, as always, he carried a long slender cane, which could, in an instant, become a harpoon, a gun, an umbrella, or a walking stick, depending on the circumstances and the weather.

Nine-year-old Roxie always looked forward to his visits, for he had traveled all over the world with Lord Thistlebottom from London. And Lord Thistlebottom was the famous author of the book *Lord Thistlebottom's Book of Pitfalls and How to Survive Them.*

"Come in! Come in!" said Roxie's father, shaking the uncle's hand and ushering him to the big easy chair with a footstool at the ready.

This time, however, instead of telling the family about his latest adventure, Uncle Dangerfoot asked, "How are you getting along with that hooligan bunch now, Roxie?"

"Well," she replied, "Helvetia doesn't try to tape my ears back anymore."

Mrs. Warbler folded her hands in her lap and smiled. "Because Roxie was the only one who could hear those robbers creeping through the forest, so what would they have done without her?"

"And Simon doesn't throw things at me anymore," said Roxie.

Her father was smiling proudly too. "Because Roxie showed them how to dig a trench and hide in it at night when those robbers came looking for them," he told Uncle Dangerfoot.

"Freddy Filch doesn't hit me anymore," said Roxie.

Mrs. Warbler made a clicking sound with her tongue. "And shameful that he ever did!" she declared. "But he'll not be hitting you again, after you were the one to slip into those robbers' tent and get food and water for the others."

"And Smoky Jo follows me wherever I go, just in case I need her," said Roxie.

"Thinks the world of our Roxie, ever since she saw her eat a bug," said Mr. Warbler with a chuckle. "Mean and sassy as those kids can be, not a one was brave enough to eat an insect if they had to."

"It was a grub," Roxie explained. "Wrapped in a dandelion leaf."

"Aha! Survival food! Page 243 of Lord Thistlebottom's book!" cried her uncle. "Jolly good!"

"So we get along," Roxie explained. "Sometimes I wish they wouldn't hang around so much, but it's better being friends than enemies."

"Absolutely," said her uncle. "And speaking of friends, I promised that you could invite a friend. Have you decided who that will be?"

"Norman!" Roxie told him. "He's been my best friend forever, and he's packed and waiting."

"Then we shall drink our tea and be off before it gets much later," said her uncle. When he had finished his crumpet, he turned to Roxie's mother: "I've hired a housekeeper for the week to watch over the children, dear sister; she'll look after Roxie's every need."

"You are so kind," Mrs. Warbler told him.

So Roxie said good-bye to her parents and carried her small suitcase to the car. The hooligans were gone now, but three blocks away, Uncle Dangerfoot stopped at the little house where Norman was waiting with his backpack. He was a chubby boy with thick glasses, who the hooligans used to tease and torment just as they had bullied Roxie.

Norman said good afternoon to Uncle Dangerfoot, tossed his backpack into the car, and climbed in beside Roxie. And soon they were on their way.

It was almost five hours later, and evening, when they reached a large old house that sat back a bit from the ocean, surrounded by scraggly trees and sea grass.

Roxie's big ears caught the sound of waves breaking onshore. She rolled down the window to smell the sea air. Though her little village of Chin-in-Hand was also not far from the ocean, it had no beach, no sand, no place for children to wade or swim; the water was cold, and there

were certainly no beach houses like this one.

Actually, she and Norman had fallen asleep on the long drive to Buzzard's Roost and on to Windswept House where they would be staying. They were a bit groggy and very stiff.

"The Widow Bitterworth lives here with her infant son," Uncle Dangerfoot said, "and I'm sure the housekeeper will have a good supper for us."

"I'd just like to stretch my legs!" Roxie said, climbing out and dragging her suitcase from the car.

"I'd like to go barefoot," Norman declared.

"Plenty of time for that," Uncle Dangerfoot said.

"Why do they call it Buzzard's Roost?" Roxie asked, looking around.

"Do you see that line of dead trees along the road?" her uncle said. "Buzzards seem to gather there, I'm told. Always have. Now, let me get my trunk from the trailer and we'll go inside."

The breeze tossed Roxie's hair up, down, and around. It was exciting to visit somewhere far from Chin-in-Hand, where times were hard and people did not get to travel much. She felt lucky to have a somewhat-famous uncle to take her places.

Uncle Dangerfoot reached for the latch on the trailer and opened the door.

"What in thunder . . . ?" he bellowed.

Roxie stared as Helvetia Hagus, Simon Surly, Freddy Filch, and Smoky Jo came tumbling out.

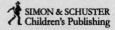